THE
FORGOTTEN LAKE
SECESSION

A NOVEL

THE
FORGOTTEN LAKE
SECESSION

A NOVEL

CHUCK BROWN

MILL CITY PRESS

Mill City Press, Inc.
2301 Lucien Way #415
Maitland, FL 32751
407.339.4217
www.millcitypublishing.com

Printed in the United States of America

ISBN: 9781545605646

ALSO BY CHUCK BROWN

FICTION
Barn Dance
The Lake Hayes Regatta
Dunn Days

NONFICTION
Letters from the attic

For Pat,
again, and with good reason!

ACKNOWLEDGMENTS

Once more my editor, Cathy Broberg, has made this a better book. Thanks also to Paul and Jan Anderson for reviewing the manuscript and offering up the back cover comment. My sister, Judy, lent her usual enthusiastic support throughout the writing as one of my readers, and thanks, of course, to Pat, my first reader and wife, for...well, everything.

PROLOGUE

The lake was like so many in Minnesota's Arrowhead region. It was nearly two miles long and a half mile wide, the surrounding forest of birch and pine growing right down to its stony shores. At its center was a rocky island, a quarter mile long and a hundred yards wide, also covered with birch and pine. In some respects it was in the middle of nowhere. Duluth and Lake Superior were an hour's drive south, while a northward hour got you to Canada. To the west was the Iron Range and to the east a wilderness of forest and lakes that one day would be preserved as the Boundary Waters Canoe Area.

The Ojibwe were the first there, and it's safe to assume that they named the lake with eloquence and imagination, as they were wont to do, though sadly no record of an Ojibwe name survived. The early Europeans arrived and looked at the lake and promptly named it Long Lake, which was neither eloquent nor imaginative—perhaps they were tired from their travels—nor did the name do anything to distinguish it from the other 150 or so Long Lakes in Minnesota.

The lake escaped the indignities of human construction until the 1930s, at which time a fellow named Floyd Baird built a log cabin on the west shore. Actually, the term "cabin" was a bit misleading, as it was an elegant two-story home with over 3,000 square feet of living space, but Floyd chose to highlight the elegance with understatement. Floyd had done rather well in the hotel business down in Minneapolis, that is until the Great Depression reversed his fortunes. Floyd's business model had always catered to high rollers—it made no sense to seek the business of those who had little money—but the hard times greatly diminished the supply of high rollers. As the vacancy rate soared at the Hotel Floyd—Floyd liked to brand his assets with his name—the bank began making menacing comments about the state of Floyd's operating loan.

"What the hell do you expect? There's a depression going on!" Floyd stammered at the bankers, hoping for compassion. Now bankers aren't much given to compassion even in good times, much less hard times, but just when foreclosure of the Floyd seemed inevitable there came a timely fire. Luckily, there was no loss of life, but the hotel was totaled.

Since a burned down Floyd suddenly make a bad loan good, the bankers merely raised their eyebrows. The insurance company, on the other hand, raised holy hell. "Arson!" they screamed. "Coincidence," Floyd shrugged.

No one really believed that the fire was coincidence, but in the end arson couldn't be proved. Floyd Baird had himself been conveniently visiting Chicago on the night of the fire, and if he had hired someone to torch the Floyd, he had hired well, so after months of foot-dragging and grumbling the insurance company finally paid up. It had been a good policy and the proceeds covered the bank loan with a tidy sum left over for Floyd. He briefly considered building a new and grander Floyd, but then he was forced to acknowledge that his enthusiasm for the hotel business and his welcome in Minneapolis had both been markedly diminished by recent events. Instead, he built his custom-designed log home on Long Lake and moved north, where he would commune with nature along with his wife, Martha, and his son, Jack. It was to be an idyllic Thoreau-like existence, albeit with a few more luxuries than old Henry David had required. The north woods would surely rekindle the passion that had once graced his marriage, while at the same time he would bond with Jack over hunting and fishing.

It didn't work out as Floyd had hoped. Martha's initial enthusiasm waned steadily through that first year as she endured buzzing clouds of mosquitoes and deer flies, poison ivy, bears and raccoons rifling through the garbage, and worst of all, cold-turkey withdrawal from a serious shopping addiction. With the onset of winter her mood only grew more sullen, despite Floyd pointing out that the cold had killed the mosquitoes and that the bears were now hibernating. Indeed, Floyd had been looking forward to winter most of all. He had envisioned still, wintry nights with a full moon illuminating the frozen snow-covered lake. Outside it would be bone-chilling cold, but the cabin would be toasty warm, and Floyd and Martha would make love in front of the fireplace on the bearskin he had bought with that in mind. Sadly, that never happened, and by mid-January Martha had taken to pacing in long flannel nightgowns with a quilt wrapped tightly about her, muttering under her breath, pausing occasionally to glare accusingly at Floyd. In February she took to lying in bed all day, weeping as she thumbed through catalogues and dreamed of shopping along Nicollet Avenue in Minneapolis. Spring came late that year—the ice didn't go off the lake until May—and by then Floyd's marriage was beyond repair.

Nor did bonding with Jack go as planned. Prior to moving north, Floyd had never really gotten to know his son. The hotel had been his life and he had left Jack's nurturing to Martha, but with his new life Floyd hoped to change all that, and to Jack's credit he took to life on the woodsy lake with gusto. He loved swimming and fishing. He was at home in the woods in every season, and though he was only seven and too young to hunt, he dreamed of the day when he would shoot his first buck. Jack was made for this life. Floyd's problem was that the more he got to know Jack, the more he realized that his son was a disagreeable little turd. The boy was demanding of attention and given to shrieking tantrums when he didn't get his own way. He had a special talent for breaking things. He had an even greater talent for losing things, especially things that belonged to Floyd. Floyd understood that Jack was his son and that he was obliged to endure much on behalf of the whiny little shit, but spending a lot of time with him no longer seemed such a compelling idea.

Not surprisingly, as Floyd's Walden Pond vision faded his entrepreneurial juices began flowing again. He started looking at the lake in a different light, much as he would a site for a new hotel. A plan, a new vision began to emerge. Of course, the biggest problem with developing real estate that was so remote was that it was ... well, so remote. It was hard to get to. The road coming up from Duluth was gravel most of the way, and for the final ten miles before Long Lake it was nothing more than wheel tracks through the woods that were often snowed shut in winter. Floyd always did his research before embarking on a business venture, and his research now was aided by an old acquaintance in St. Paul who happened to work for the state of Minnesota. It seemed that the state was looking to accommodate its growing lumber industry, and with that in mind it planned to upgrade the road from Duluth to a paved two-lane highway all the way to Garner Lake, just fifteen miles south of Long Lake. The upgrade was to commence three years hence, and better yet, the following year it was to be extended all the way to Long Lake. None of this was for public knowledge, the St. Paul acquaintance cautioned. It was still in the planning stage and subject to change, though he did put the probability of the project going ahead at eighty percent.

Eighty percent was good enough for Floyd. He reckoned that those who waited for one hundred percent too often found that the train had left the station when they finally got there. The time to strike was now. The country was still in the grips of the Great Depression, so land could be bought dirt cheap by those having the wherewithal. Floyd not only had the wherewithal, he was also armed with the knowledge of the coming highway, knowledge the other landowners didn't have. Floyd's cabin had been the first on the lake, and since then a few smaller cabins and hunting shacks had gone up, but the vast majority of the land was still undeveloped. Better still, it was all privately owned; there were no public lands around the lake, so Floyd wouldn't have to deal with government bureaucrats, only unsuspecting souls who had no idea as to the future value of their property.

It was like taking candy from a baby. The depression-weary owners nearly tripped over one another in their rush to swap their land for Floyd's cash, and in less than two years he owned every inch of property around the lake and the entire island too. With the land sewed up, Floyd then turned to refining his new vision for Long Lake. Ever the optimist, he foresaw the end of the depression and the return of good times. With new prosperity people would want places to play, which Floyd meant to provide. Much of the land would be designated as lots for cabins, which would markedly increase the population around the lake. Having more people around would in turn benefit the other enterprises Floyd had in mind. There would be a shopping complex that sold groceries and liquor and gas and hunting and fishing supplies. Of course there would be a gift shop. At the lake's south end he planned to build a resort, complete with main lodge and individual cabins, a restaurant or two, and possibly a golf course. The island offered intriguing possibilities too, and he toyed with yet another resort, a smaller more exclusive one, aimed at some well-heeled subset of society, nudists perhaps. Long Lake would indeed become a grand destination, high rollers would surely flock there, and Floyd, per his usual custom, personally branded it by changing the name to Lake Floyd.

"Can you do that?" Martha wondered. "I mean, can you just go around renaming geographical places?"

"Why the hell not?" Floyd said. "I own the whole goddamn thing. I can call it whatever I want."

"But what about the maps? All the maps say Long Lake."

"So they'll make new maps," Floyd said, realizing it had been a waste of time to share his vision with Martha. The woman's own visions were always clouded by mosquitoes and bears and the like. Floyd, on the other hand, saw the future clearly, and he looked smugly forward to all the profits his Lake Floyd ventures would earn.

As it turned out, Floyd didn't foresee the future quite as accurately as he thought. Most notably, he missed World War II. After the Japanese attacked Pearl Harbor, life in America changed dramatically, and along with it Floyd's prospects. The war effort stimulated the economy and people once more had money, but nothing to spend it on other than war bonds. No cars or appliances were manufactured. Houses weren't built, much less lake cabins. All resources were directed to making the machinery of war. Worse still, the state of Minnesota postponed indefinitely the plan to improve the road up from Duluth.

"What about the lumber?" Floyd sputtered. "How you gonna get the logs out?"

The state officials pointed west toward the Iron Range. "More important we get the ore out. This war's going to be won with steel. And eventually we'll do the road. Just not now."

"When?" demanded Floyd.

The officials offered a collective shrug. "You tell us how long the war will last, then add, say, five years to that, and that should get you close."

So there it was. Floyd had invested everything he had in real estate he now had no hope of developing for years to come. It felt as if he had been personally targeted. Oh, sure, there was a war on, but to Floyd's way of thinking it still smacked of a conspiracy between Japan and the state of Minnesota, a conspiracy to ruin Floyd Baird. His old insurance company was probably involved too. In the end, Floyd had no choice but to return to the sprawling log cabin on the lake that he shared with his bitchy wife and his whiny kid, but that didn't mean his good name had to be associated with it. In a fit of pique that was long on irony, he changed the name again. What had once been Long Lake, then Lake Floyd, would now be known as Forgotten Lake.

CHAPTER 1

Cass Baird was reading in her New Orleans apartment when the ringtone sounded on her cell phone. She picked it up and looked at the screen, saw who was calling and was tempted to let it go to voice mail, but then guilt prevailed.

"Hello, Mother."

Without preamble Diane Baird said, "Well, I did it. I finally left him."

Cass sighed. She understood what her mother was saying, that she had separated from her father, something she'd been threatening for years. Now that it was done, Cass searched for something appropriate to say, and when she couldn't think of anything she simply asked, "Why?"

"Why? Why?" Diane Baird said, her voice rising. "Why not, for God's sake? Forty-two years of marriage to Jack Baird is more than enough reason all by itself. Frankly, I've been a saint for suffering it as long as I have."

Cass resisted snickering at the notion of long-suffering sainthood for her mother. "Well, he must've done something to bring this on."

"Of course, he did. Forty-two years of his bullheadedness and goofy ideas is what brought it on. Look, Cassandra, you haven't been home in a while. You have no idea how bad it's gotten. I tell you, the man's gone round the bend and he's not coming back."

"So you're not at the lake?"

"Of course, I'm not at the lake. I told you, I left him."

"Then where are you?"

"Minneapolis."

"Alone?"

Diane Baird hesitated. "I'm staying with a friend."

"Oh. Anyone I know?"

Another hesitation. "If you must know, I've moved in with someone. A gentleman."

"Ah, a gentleman. Is this someone you've known for long?"

"Don't take that tone with me, Cassandra. I've actually known Gerald for a good while, but there's never been anything ... improper about it. He's a true gentleman. And now he's my savior. You'll see when you meet him."

"And where does Gerald live?"

"Right downtown. In a condo overlooking the river. It's really quite elegant and *so* civilized compared to that godforsaken lake. Here, I'll give you the address."

Cass wrote down the address as her mother rattled it off; then she said, "Thanks for letting me know, Mother, but I am sorry to hear the news."

"Don't be. Feeling sorry about your father is a waste of time. And speaking of time, I have to go. Gerald and I are going out to dinner, then to the theater. When was the last time your father did anything like that?"

"There's not a lot of theater at Forgotten Lake, Mother."

"Tell me about it," said Diane Baird. "Come see me soon. You must meet Gerald. And you'll love the view. Good-bye." With that she broke the connection.

Cass sat staring at her phone as a weight of sadness settled over her. Her parents' separation hadn't come as a surprise. Given the fractiousness of their marriage, the surprise was that they stayed together as long as they did, but their separation now threatened Cass's sense of home. And no matter where Cass lived, or how long she was away, Forgotten Lake would always be home. She had grown up there. All her childhood memories were there, and despite her parents' rocky marriage, she'd had a happy childhood. Her mother had been right when she said that Cass hadn't been home in a while, but that did nothing to lessen her vivid recollections of sparkling blue water and pine-scented air, or the call of a loon across the moonlit lake. Nor could time erase her memories of hiking in the woods or fishing for panfish with her father in a small rowboat. Forgotten Lake had always been the place her soul's compass unerringly pointed to from anywhere else on earth, but now for the first time in her life her true north seemed in doubt.

She looked out her third-floor apartment window to Bourbon Street, sweltering below in the July heat. Bourbon Street, party central in the Big Easy, was a marked contrast to Forgotten Lake in so many ways. Every day in the French Quarter was a feast of music and food and boozy revelry, a unique sensory overload. Cass's apartment was on a more residential stretch of the street, making it a bit quieter, but no less exotic. She had been in New Orleans for nearly four years now, and while she still hadn't gotten used to the clammy heat, she loved everything else about the city. She thought of her life there as her walk on the wild side, a life differing not just from Forgotten Lake, but also from her day job, which was adjunct professor of economics at Tulane University.

Cass's journey from Forgotten Lake to Tulane had been a nomadic one, as academic careers often are. She had done her undergraduate and graduate work at the University of Minnesota, then took a series of teaching positions in state colleges, first in the Midwest, then on the East Coast, followed by the West Coast. Tulane was clearly her most prestigious stop thus far, though a full professorship seemed a distant hope, if ever. Each month she had to stretch her adjunct's salary to cover the cost of living in the Quarter, but she got by, and now at the age of forty she had settled into a comfortable midlife existence in which she avoided worries about the future simply by not thinking about it. Among friends, she often joked that she had become a spinster schoolteacher, though that description didn't really fit. She was a pleasantly attractive woman

3

who had maintained her figure through regular visits to the gym. Her current choice of hair color was honey blonde, and while she preferred blue jeans over high fashion, she wore her jeans well. No, Cass Baird didn't look the spinster, and though she'd never married, she'd had her share of lovers over the years. There had even been one proposal of marriage, but it hadn't felt right, and looking back she often wondered if her saying "no" had as much to do with her family history as the man in question. Her grandparents, Floyd and Martha, had fought as much as her parents, and it almost seemed as if the Baird clan was doomed to unhappy marriages.

And now her parents' marriage had ended, her mother shacked up with Gentleman Gerald, her father apparently gone round the bend at Forgotten Lake, though Cass couldn't bring herself to believe that last part. Jack Baird was eccentric, to be sure, and certainly difficult to live with, but to Cass it seemed that he had always had an iron grip on reality, and it was hard to imagine him losing that grip. She had usually avoided taking sides in her parents' spats, but in truth Cass's sympathy had mostly gone to her father. Perhaps that was because he felt the same way she did about Forgotten Lake, while her mother had never bothered to conceal her contempt for their life there. And now, with any pretense of family solidarity dashed once and for all, Cass felt the sudden, strong pull of Forgotten Lake. A broken home, yes, but home nonetheless.

It was late July. She had wrapped up her summer session class at Tulane the week before, and the fall semester didn't start for over a month. There was nothing to keep her in New Orleans, and now so many reasons—including the heat—to leave. It was an easy decision. The next morning she would climb in her car and drive out of the city with the hope that she could still find her true north.

CHAPTER 2

$\mathcal{J}$ack Baird sat on the deck of his log home, sipping his morning coffee and watching the sun burn the mist off Forgotten Lake. This was how most of his days began and he couldn't imagine a more peaceful start. Even if the hours ahead brought trouble—and they often did—he could deal with it, safe in the knowledge that the next morning would surely come and once more grant him solace on the lake and a new beginning. Lately there had been an added quality to his morning peace, a sense of freedom that had coincided with his wife's departure for Minneapolis. Whatever it was that had once passed for love in their marriage had long since given way to a weary indulgence. The shift hadn't happened all at once but had rather come on slowly like the arthritis in his shoulder, something to be tolerated. Well, he still had the pain in his shoulder, but Diane Baird was gone, and with her absence had come a sense of relief and freedom. As it turned out, he didn't need her at all. He could look after himself perfectly well, and he'd long known that he was the better cook of the two. Even his morning coffee was now strong enough for his tastes, after years of suffering through her tepid brew.

In most respects, Jack's new life differed little from his married life. The center of his world had always been Forgotten Lake, and he asked nothing more than to be left alone there, alone to fish and hunt, or tramp through the woods, or simply sit on his deck and stare at the water. He had never gotten along with his father and he certainly hadn't acquired Floyd Baird's entrepreneurial zeal. He had always resisted any thought of developing the land around Forgotten Lake, as having neighbors who would undoubtedly pry into his business were the very last thing he wanted. The only exceptions were two tiny cabins—shacks really—on the other side of the lake owned by characters even more reclusive than Jack. Diane Baird had derisively called them Jack's minions, but they were all the company he needed. Jack lived modestly and to make ends meet, he cobbled together part-time work here and there that didn't interfere with his hunting and fishing. He was good with his hands and had often worked as a carpenter, helping build a number of cabins and lake homes on area lakes, but of course never on Forgotten Lake.

None of this was to suggest that Jack's new bachelor life was trouble free. To the contrary, it often seemed as if trouble came looking for him, though Diane had claimed it was the other way around—that Jack sought it out. Whatever the case, Jack had the look of a man who could handle trouble. At eighty years old, he still had a full head of hair, now snowy white, his face tanned and creased from years in the elements. He was average in height, but his body was still lean and wiry, his scarred, gnarled hands strong, his blue eyes clear and sharp. Yes, definitely a man made for trouble.

Indeed, trouble seemed to be the Baird family's natural state, and Jack had learned a thing or two from Floyd Baird about dealing with it. First of all, always look out for Number One, because you can't expect anyone else to do it. And secondly, trouble was most likely to come from the government or lawyers or insurance companies, if not necessarily in that order. Sure enough, Jack's current trouble involved the government, though there remained the possibility that lawyers and insurance companies would join in before it all played out.

It had all started innocently enough earlier that summer when Jack banged his aluminum fishing boat into a rock, severely denting the hull. That boat was one of Jack's prized possessions, so he took the dent personally. Making matters worse, a week later he hit another rock, tearing up the propeller on his outboard motor. Now Jack and rocks had coexisted peacefully on Forgotten Lake for years, but that relationship was now being strained by the second dry year in a row. The lake's water level was nearing an all-time low, and rocks that Jack had never known about suddenly posed a mighty threat. Something had to be done. Removing the offending rocks was the sort of herculean task that, once started, would never end. Better to solve the problem in a natural way, or as Jack put it, in the beaver way.

The Bumble River meandered through miles of bog and woods before flowing into the north end of Forgotten Lake, then exiting through an outlet at the south end. Calling the Bumble a river was an act of aggrandizement in normal times, and in a dry period such as this it slowed to a mere trickle. Still, it was Forgotten Lake's chief tributary and the best means of raising the lake level, providing a dam was constructed at the south outlet. The dam that Jack built was a fine one indeed. He drove steel posts deep into the ground on both sides of the outlet; then he closed off the flow with a two-by-twelve plank. Not exactly the Hoover Dam, but the right dam for Forgotten Lake. Jack's goal was to raise the water level a foot, which he calculated would protect his boat and motor from most of the lake's rocks without unduly threatening the shoreline with erosion. Sure enough, the lake began slowly rising, and after a few weeks and some timely rain it was up six inches. That's when the trouble started.

The fellow arrived at Jack's place in a shiny new four-wheel-drive pickup. The fellow looked all shiny and new, too, in his creased khakis and polo shirt with a clipboard in his hand. The pickup had tax exempt plates, which meant it was a government vehicle, which meant that Jack's taxes had helped pay for it. True, Jack didn't pay a lot of taxes, but he paid enough to resent government guys driving shiny new pickups while he drove an old battered one that was starting to rust. Jack eyed the fellow warily as he walked up with a cocky grin on his face.

"Mr. Baird?" The fellow offered his hand to Jack. "I'm Brian Walsh with the County Soil and Water Conservation District."

This news did nothing to ease Jack's wariness, and he left Walsh standing with his hand extended for an awkward moment before giving it a quick shake. "What's your business?"

"It's about your dam, Mr. Baird."

"What about it?"

"Well, you don't have a permit for it."

Jack nodded his agreement. "So?"

"So your dam's illegal. You have to remove it."

"Ain't gonna happen," Jack said. "That dam's on private land, land that I happen to own, and I don't see how it's anybody else's business."

The cocky grin had disappeared from Walsh's face. "Well, that's a problem, Mr. Baird. We're talking about a flowing body of water, and property owners downstream have rights too. It *is* other people's business."

"How'd you find out about my dam, anyhow?"

"Actually, we had a complaint from a downstream property owner about an interrupted flow, so I checked it out and found your dam."

"You trespassed on my property?"

"No, Mr. Baird, I'm authorized to enter your property in the performance of my job. Now granted, I can't go in your house looking for a dam, but I can sure check out your stream. The law's clear on that."

"We'll just see about that. Who's this downstream asshole that ratted me out?"

"Actually, I don't know. The complaint was made to someone else in our office, but I wouldn't tell you if I did know. Feuds between property owners accomplish nothing. We just want everyone to obey the law, and the law says your dam's gotta go."

"What if I apply for a permit?"

"You can certainly do that, but I'll tell you right now that it's a very involved process and in the end they hardly ever get approved. If you were, say, the Tennessee Valley Authority, it might be different, but you're just Jack Baird, so your odds aren't that good."

Jack snorted. "I may not be no Tennessee whatever, but I ain't that easy to push around. What if I just refuse to take it out? What you gonna do about it then?"

Walsh sighed. "I truly hope it won't come to that, but if it does, we'll get a court order directing the sheriff to remove it."

Jack nodded in silence for a long moment. "Seems like we've come to something of a standoff here, so it's probably best for you to get the hell off my land along about now."

Walsh looked as though he was about to say something more; then he thought better of it and simply shrugged before turning and walking to his truck.

Now Jack drained the last gulp of coffee from his mug and contemplated what to do with the rest of his day. Taking the boat out on the lake and trolling for walleyes was certainly an option, one that he often chose, and the day seemed perfect for it. The sun felt warm on his back and a light breeze was rippling across the water. Yes, a good day to be on the lake, and while he was out there he could motor to the south end and check on his dam.

It had been a month since Brian Walsh's visit, and since then a sheriff's deputy and two fellas from the county highway department had come out and removed the dam—twice! Jack had been encouraged the second time when they didn't seem at all upset about having to come back and do the job again. It had probably helped that Jack had met them with a thermos of coffee and a box of doughnuts. Hospitality helped to work out differences, and like the deputy said, it's always nice working around a lake. That had set a proper tone. Conflict, in Jack's view, was less troublesome if the participants just didn't get so damn angry.

Jack expected them back any day now, and he was ready for them. He had taken his pickup to town and laid in a supply of two-by-twelve planks and steel posts, enough to keep playing the game until the lake froze over in November. Of course, the lake level fell again every time the dam came out, so Jack still had rock problems, but he didn't mind so much now that he had the dam game to play with the county guys. It was good to be busy. When a fella gets to be eighty, Jack reasoned, he needs something to occupy his time or he'll start feeling old, sure as hell.

CHAPTER 3

The St. Louis County Soil and Water Conservation District maintained an office for the northern half of the county in Forsythe, Minnesota, a town of some ten thousand people. Brian Walsh was at his desk there, working on a report, when Zack Buchwald, the office manager, came by.

"Is that dam on Forgotten Lake taken care of?" Buchwald asked.

"It will be. I talked to the sheriff's office today, and they're going back out there …" Brian paused to consult notes on his desk. "Day after tomorrow."

"Bullshit! Call 'em back and tell 'em it's gotta be done tomorrow."

"I'm not sure they'll appreciate us dictating their schedule, Zack."

"I don't give a shit. I want it out tomorrow. And this time I want it to stay out. Who the hell's that guy think he is, anyway?"

"Might not be that easy. Baird seems like a pretty stubborn guy."

"That's your problem. Get the judge to throw his ass in jail for contempt of court. Just do whatever you gotta do."

Brian leaned back in his chair and paused a moment before giving voice to what he had been thinking the past few days. "You know, Zack, from a lake management point of view, a dam on the outlet of Forgotten Lake isn't such a bad idea. Maybe we oughta see if we can help Baird get a permit."

"Not such a bad idea, eh? Well, let me tell you why it's a very bad idea. County Commissioner Dugan just happens to own some land along the Bumble south of Forgotten Lake, and County Commissioner Dugan has been calling every day to ask how the hell he's supposed to catch trout in a stream that doesn't have enough water to float a goddamn minnow? That's why Baird's dam is a bad idea, and that's why you're gonna make sure he doesn't put it in again."

Ah, politics, thought Brian. Politics will trump a good idea every time. He had known that a downstream property owner had complained about the flow on the Bumble, but until now he hadn't known the complainer's identity. Having a county commissioner involved certainly put things in a different light, and it also explained Zack Buchwald's keen interest. Zack always leaned whichever way the political winds were blowing.

After Zack left, Brian picked up his phone and called the sheriff's area office in Forsythe, asking for Deputy Skinner. When Skinner came on the line, Brian asked, "Sam, any chance you can do that Forgotten Lake dam tomorrow?"

"Tomorrow? Might be tough. I've got some papers to serve, and even if I could work around that, I still need a couple highway department boys to help out, and those people over there don't like anyone dicking with their schedule. Probably best to stay with the day after tomorrow."

Brian wasn't surprised. "Well, at least get it done first thing in the morning."

Sam Skinner hesitated a moment. "Might be closer to mid-morning, Brian."

"Why's that?"

"Well, that's about when me and the boys would normally take a break, and old Jack likes to come around with coffee and doughnuts."

"How does he even know you're there?"

"Oh, we stop at his place first to let him know we're gonna be on his property. It's a courtesy thing, you know."

Yeah, thought Brian, a courtesy thing that also happens to ensure that the landowner shows up with coffee and doughnuts. "Look, Sam, the powers over here are getting pretty impatient with this whole business. What do you think it'll take to convince Baird not to put it in again?"

"Hard to say, Brian. I get the impression that he's just having a bunch of fun with the whole damn thing."

"Well, fun or not, there is a court order involved, and he could wind up in jail for contempt."

"Aw, geez, I hope it doesn't come to that. I'd like to think we got better things to do."

After hanging up the phone, Brian sat there and pondered having better things to do. To be sure, he'd rather not be dealing with what he'd come to think of as the Rumble on the Bumble. On the one hand was a harmless old guy, a little goofy maybe, but likeable enough, enough so that even the deputy sheriff sent out to correct his ways ended up taking his side. Now on the other hand appears Commissioner Dugan who wants to go trout fishing in the worst way and was willing to exert his considerable clout to see that it happened. Caught in the middle was Brian Walsh, program coordinator for the county's Soil and Water Conservation District, and he understood only too well that when the shit starts to fly, whoever is in the middle is likely to get hit. The irony of it was that two years earlier, at the age of forty, Brian had made a midlife career change precisely to get away from shit.

Brian had grown up in Duluth and at an early age he had fallen in love with Minnesota's Arrowhead country, with its forests and lakes and streams, and of course the region's most dominant natural resource: Lake Superior. At the University of Minnesota in Minneapolis he studied engineering, and after graduation he became a licensed civil engineer. He saw civil engineering as a way to combine his talents with his passion, a way to create harmony between the wilderness and humanity's necessary footprints there. He dreamed of a job designing those eco-friendly footprints, but unfortunately engineering jobs of that description were scarce. Instead, employment opportunity led him to a large Minneapolis firm that provided engineering services to municipalities over a three-state area. Rather than engineering harmony between nature and humanity, he spent his days sitting at a computer, designing sanitary sewers and treatment plants. Oh, he understood the importance of good sanitary systems to public health and economic vitality, but that didn't stop him, after a few beers, from claiming the job title of shit engineer. Still, it was a good job, and usually satisfying, and though the longing to ply his trade in the North Country never went away, the thing that precipitated his career change at age forty was a different kind of shit.

Kelly was the producer of the evening news at a Twin Cities TV station. Brian had known her since college, but they hadn't started dating until they were in their thirties; then dating soon led to a shared apartment. It was an arrangement that had more to do with economics and convenience than matters of the heart, but despite its casualness, Brian thought it a serious relationship that would take on a sense of permanence and commitment over time. But then, after six years together, Los Angeles happened.

"I'm moving to L.A.," she announced out of the blue one day.

"You're doing what?" Brian said, shocked.

"I got an offer from a station in Los Angeles. Bigger market, bigger job, no way I can turn it down."

"I ... I didn't know you were looking."

She shrugged. "I'm always looking."

"Well ... what about us? You're gonna split just like that?"

She shrugged again. "So come to L.A. with me. They probably have a bigger shit market too. You can do your thing out there just as well as you can do it here, maybe better."

So much for permanence. Six years together and Kelly's only commitment was to her job. Why hadn't he seen that coming? Perhaps because he wasn't committed either? In any event, he wasn't going to Los Angeles, not with someone likely to move on again at the next career opportunity, but the whole thing did cause him to take a serious look at his own life. It was clear now that he hadn't been committed to Kelly any more than she to him, but she at least was committed to her career, and it was now equally clear that Brian lacked even that. He was just going through the motions at work.

Connect the usual components—sanitary sewers and lift stations and treatment plants—then move on to the next shitty job. It was time for a change; it was time to commit to something.

A civil engineering job bringing harmony to the North Country still proved elusive, but Brian was able to land a job with the Soil and Water Conservation District. The position didn't call for a civil engineer, nor did it pay for one, but it got him away from sewers and out in the woods and on the water, places that he loved. And the job did entail a harmony of sorts. On his good days he worked as a problem solver, helping private property owners deal with state and local government and the maze of land use and environmental regulations. On those days he felt like a man on a white horse, but other days not so much, and this was one of those other days. Too often the problem he tried to solve turned into a pissing match between two property owners, and when one of the property owners turned out to be a county commissioner, as was the case with the Rumble on the Bumble, then politics only made matters worse. And now Brian found his sympathies going to Jack Baird, not Commissioner Dugan, and that wasn't smart, jobwise.

CHAPTER 4

$\mathcal{C}$ass Baird almost didn't recognize her own mother. For one thing, Diane Baird was now a blonde. For another, she'd lost weight and looked trim and fit, a result of the personal trainer Gentleman Gerald had insisted she have. Diane was in her late sixties, more than ten years younger than Cass's father, and now that age difference seemed even more pronounced. But there was more, something harder to define. It was as if Diane had acquired a new aura, a new outlook on life, or put more crudely, Cass thought, her mother had landed in money and was putting on airs.

The money part was obvious. They were seated in Gerald's downtown Minneapolis condo. The exterior wall was floor-to-ceiling glass, affording a spectacular view looking up the Mississippi River to the Stone Arch Bridge and to the Falls of St. Anthony beyond. The furnishings were equally elegant. And as Cass sat with her mother and Gerald leisurely sipping white wine at three in the afternoon, she thought her mother's new world was as far removed from Forgotten Lake as she could imagine.

Gerald himself wasn't nearly as impressive as his condo, though Cass had to admit he seemed very much the gentleman. She had arrived two hours earlier for a fashionably late lunch, and Gerald had been a genial and charming host. Still, Cass couldn't get past her first impression, which was one of softness. Not that softness was necessarily bad, it's just that she wasn't used to quite so much of it in a man. He was short and small in stature, and he had greeted her with a soft, limp hand. He also spoke in a soft voice, and his chosen attire that day of a pink cashmere sweater did nothing to add a sense of grit. It struck Cass that her mother was shacked up with a man as different from her father as the man's condo was from the cabin at Forgotten Lake.

Gerald had just excused himself and retired to his den where business matters awaited him. Diane Baird had watched him go, then seeming to sense her daughter's thoughts, said, "You really must take time to get to know Gerald, and once you do, you'll see that he's quite an extraordinary man."

"I'm sure he is, Mother. What does he do, anyway?"

"Do?"

"Well, yeah." Cass waved her hand at their surroundings. "This place is pretty impressive, and I suppose it's tacky to ask, but how does he come by it?"

Diane paused for a sip of wine. "It's not as if Gerald has to trundle off to the office every day and *do* anything. It's more a matter of being *from* money."

"Ah, from. So where does the money that he's from come from?"

"And yes, you are being tacky, but I suppose you've got some right to know, though truth be told, I don't really understand it myself. Gerald's grandfather did something or other with soybeans. I really couldn't tell you what, but it involved processing plants and that sort of thing, quite a lot of it too. At any rate, those things are still somehow involved, but Gerald doesn't deal with any of it directly. He works with trusts and foundations, things like that, though I couldn't begin to tell you how it all works." She paused for a shrug. "It's the sort of things you *economists* go on about."

Cass noted the emphasis on the word "economist." Her mother had always deemed Cass's profession to be an odd choice for a woman, but Cass opted now to avoid reopening that argument. All past efforts to explain her love of the discipline had ended with Diane saying something like, "But it's all so dreary. I should think fashion would be much more interesting."

"But however he comes by his money," Diane said, "you have to admit this place is quite a step up from the cabin on that godforsaken lake."

Cass just shrugged, avoiding another argument.

"There's also a Florida condo on Marco Island, and another in Aspen."

"My, my, Marco Island and Aspen. I'm so happy for you, Mother."

Diane glared at her daughter. "I don't appreciate your tone one bit, Cassandra. And it's not just about condos and things. I finally have a life. I meet interesting people, fascinating people, all the time. That never happened at that godforsaken lake. Up there I could go weeks and the only people I'd see were your father and his stupid minions. Believe me, that's no kind of life."

Cass smiled. "So Dad's minions are still around?"

"Oh, yes, and revolting as ever."

"That's awfully strong, don't you think? I mean Dup's pretty harmless."

"Harmless, maybe, but Dup Dingle is still a revolting, disgusting little man. And I certainly wouldn't call Hamilton Madison harmless."

"Ham still claiming to be a direct descendant from James Madison?"

"Of course. And lately he's decided that makes him a one-man defender of the Constitution."

Cass chuckled.

"It's not funny, Cassandra. That man sees a threat to the Constitution lurking behind every tree. He comes up with a new conspiracy every week, and one of these days he's either going to shoot someone or someone's going to shoot him." Diane thought a moment. "The latter would be the better outcome, of course."

"Sounds like old times at Forgotten Lake."

"And then there's your father. He's taken to picking fights with the county and the state, and I suppose the feds'll be next."

"What's that all about?"

"This ridiculous dam he seems to think the lake needs. He keeps putting it in and the county keeps taking it out. It's utter madness. If you ask me, they're all a bunch of fools."

Cass sipped wine rather than commenting. It came as no surprise that, given her mother's new view of the world from Gentleman Gerald's condo, she would see fools everywhere. Cass had a sudden urge to be somewhere else, a sudden urge to get to Forgotten Lake as quickly as possible. "Well, this has been very nice, Mother. I love your view, but I suppose I should be going."

"But you just got here."

"Yes, but I'm hoping to get up to the lake tonight."

"Well, you can't do that. For one thing, you've been drinking wine all afternoon. You're in no condition to drive. And for another, Gerald's taking us out to a lovely French restaurant tonight. It'll probably be the last good meal you'll get in a while since you seem determined to go up and expose yourself to your father's fried everything."

Cass started to protest, but Diane cut her off. "You'll go out to dinner with us and you'll stay in our guest room tonight, and that's final. For the life of me, I don't understand how you can be in such a hurry to get back to the godforsaken lake."

Yes, Cass was in a hurry to get to the lake, in a hurry to get home, but she knew better than to try to explain why to her mother.

CHAPTER 5

*J*ack Baird thought of it as his happy place. It was a two-foot by five-foot shelf, covered with Formica and nailed waist high between two birch trees at the side of his log home. It was Jack's fish cleaning station. It was where he stood to fillet his catch, a satisfying experience in itself, a satisfaction that rose to the level of happiness by the fact that he could look out onto Forgotten Lake as he worked. On this day there was much to be happy about. He had caught two nice walleyes, both about eighteen inches long, and as he cleaned them he kept glancing at the lake, which was doing itself particularly proud. A light breeze rippled the blue water beneath a cloudless sky as the afternoon sun reflected a path of diamonds across the lake's surface to the pine- and birch-covered island beyond. It was a sight worthy of a beer ad, and with nice fish added to the mix it was a sure recipe for happiness.

The magic was then broken by the sound of an outboard motor, and Jack looked up as a small aluminum boat with a single occupant rounded the southern tip of the island and steered toward his dock. The boat slowed as it came near and bumped to a stop along the dock. The occupant, a man, scrambled out and tied the boat off, then made his way to shore.

Jack continued filleting as the man approached; then without looking up, he said, "Afternoon, Dup."

19

"Hey, Jack," Dup Dingle said. "Looks like you got a couple nice ones."

"Ain't complaining."

"I was out earlier, but all I got was a couple small perch."

Jack looked up now. Dup Dingle was never much to look at, and today was no exception. He was a small man, only five and a half feet tall, with narrow shoulders and a sunken chest that gave way to a small potbelly. His baggy jeans had a tear in one knee and a rope served as his belt. This day he wore a plain gray T-shirt, though in cooler weather he usually added a wrinkled flannel shirt. It was his standard attire, and while it lacked style, it was reasonably clean, as he diligently did laundry every Saturday, the same day he reserved for bathing. Saturday was also for shaving, and since it was midweek he sported several days' worth of salt-and-pepper stubble. Jack wasn't sure of Dup's age—he doubted that Dup himself knew with any accuracy—but he guessed him to be about fifty, though that could easily have varied ten years either way. He lived alone in a one-room cabin, a shack really, on the other side of the lake, his only other possessions of note being his boat and motor and an old pickup that hadn't run for several years. Despite his mean appearance, Dup was a happy man with a ready smile, a toothy grin that revealed fewer teeth with each passing year.

"So what're you up to today?" Jack asked.

Dup looked down and shuffled his feet, which is what he usually did when he was about to ask a favor. "Well, I was wondering if you was thinking a going to town today?"

"Wasn't planning on it."

"How 'bout tomorrow?"

"Maybe. What've you got in mind?"

"Well, see, I cut up a bunch a deadfall birch in back of my place, and old Henry in town told me that if I ever got a pickup load a birch, he'd pay me a hundred and twenty bucks for it."

"You're turning into quite the capitalist, Dup," Jack said with a mischievous grin.

Dup paused here, as if to wonder what the term "capitalist" had to do with the matters at hand. "Anyway, I got me a pickup load a birch, but I ain't got a pickup to haul it in, and I was thinking if you was going to town, then maybe we could load the birch in your pickup."

Jack received this in silence as he continued filleting fish. Disinterest, he had learned, was a most effective bargaining tool.

After an uneasy moment, Dup stepped up the negotiations. "You can have the twenty bucks and I'll just keep the hundred."

"Twenty bucks? That's all my pickup's worth?"

"Well, hell, Jack, I done cut up all that wood. Took me most of a day. I figure that oughta be worth at least a hundred. Besides, it's only five miles into town."

"What do you need a hundred bucks for anyway?" Jack said. He enjoyed needling Dup and he only felt a little guilty about it. "You wouldn't know what to do with a hundred bucks."

"Hell, I wouldn't."

"Oh, yeah? If you had a hundred bucks right now, what would you do with it?"

Dup sighed as he contemplated the possibilities. "If I had me a hundred bucks, I'd go to Duluth and get me some beer. Then I'd get me a room at the Radisson, and then I'd get me a hooker and have her set on my face for a spell, and then I'd have her give me a blow job, and then—"

"Whoa, hold on there, Dup. I think the beer and the Radisson more'n took care of your hundred bucks."

Dup's shoulders sagged and his expression turned forlorn, the look of a man longing for a life he couldn't afford.

"You know, Dup, if you were a real capitalist, you'd take that hundred bucks and make a down payment on a chainsaw. Then you could really cut some wood."

"I don't wanna be no fucking capitalist," Dup said, defiant now. "I just wanna go to Duluth and get me a hooker."

Jack chuckled. He doubted that Dup had been to Duluth in the past five years, and for that matter, he suspected that Dup might well be a fifty-something virgin. He rarely left his reclusive shack on the lake, and given his sorry appearance, women weren't likely to come around seeking his company. On top of all that, Jack knew for a fact that Dup kept a moss box on a shelf in his shack. It was a simple wooden box, a foot long and four inches square and open on one end. Dup kept it stuffed with fresh moss gathered from the surrounding woods, and while Jack never pressed Dup on its exact function, he suspected that it served as a substitute vagina. It was pretty sad, really, but on the other hand, when Jack considered his own failings at marital bliss, the moss box wasn't completely without merit. If it was Dup's lot in life to forgo a complete woman and get by with only a simulated part, then at least he had chosen one of the more desirable parts, a part not likely to demand that Dup change his ways or take up religion.

"So can we haul my wood to town in your pickup or not?" Dup said now.

Jack decided that he had needled Dup enough for one day. "I suppose. I gotta go into town tomorrow morning anyway, so I'll swing by your place first, but you're gonna do all the loading and unloading. I ain't tossing no goddamn logs."

"No problem, Jack. And for you trouble I'll gladly pay you ten bucks."

"Twenty. You said twenty."

"Well, that was if you helped with the loading and unloading."

"You ain't in any position to negotiate, Dup. You want me to haul your wood to town, it'll cost you twenty bucks. And if you don't agree to that right now, it might cost you thirty."

"Oh, alright," Dup agreed to the terms as the sound of tires crunching gravel was heard from the back of the house. Both men turned to look as a woman climbed from the car that had just parked there. "Hey, Jack," Dup said, "you got some pussy coming to visit."

Jack shook his head in disgust. "That ain't no pussy, you dumb shit. That's my daughter."

* * *

Cass Baird felt great contentment. She was seated at the big oak table in the Baird family log home, sipping scotch on the rocks. The entire lake side of the house consisted of a long great room beneath a vaulted ceiling, with French doors and large windows providing unrestricted views of the lake. At the far end was a stone fireplace and around that an arrangement of several overstuffed chairs and a sofa. In the middle of the room a staircase led up to an open, railed walkway running the length of the house, connecting to the master suite and two other bedrooms. Beneath those rooms and at the back of the house were a guest suite and a den. The open kitchen area was at the end opposite the living area, near the table where Cass sat. The walls and ceiling were done in gleaming knotty pine throughout, lending a warmth to defy even the coldest winter night. Despite the size, the place still felt like a cabin, a cozy harmony with the surrounding lake and woods, a sense of the outdoors brought inside and still offering shelter. It was a far cry from a high-rise condo overlooking the Mississippi River in Minneapolis, nor did it boast a large supply of expensive wine, but Cass was happy with the scotch and beer provided. She was home and that's what mattered.

And now, best of all, came the spatter and sizzle of fat as her father began dropping chunks of beer-battered walleye into a pot of hot oil a few feet away in the kitchen. New Orleans was home to some of the world's finest cuisine, and Cass truly loved it, but Jack Baird's deep-fried walleye was her ultimate home food.

"You've no idea how much I've been looking forward to this meal," Cass said.

Jack paused for a sip of his own scotch before saying, "Lucky thing I caught a couple nice ones today."

"Right, as if you don't have about ten pounds of the stuff stashed away in your freezer."

He grinned. "Well, I like being prepared for all contingencies."

"It was fun to see Dup today," she said, changing the subject. "He hasn't changed a bit."

Jack shook his head. "The words 'Dup Dingle' and 'change' ain't ever gonna happen in the same sentence."

"And how's Ham? I heard he's taking his hereditary role as defender of the Constitution more seriously than ever."

Jack spooned fried walleye onto a platter lined with paper towels to absorb the excess fat; then he added more raw fish to the pot before looking up at Cass. "You heard that, huh? Like maybe from your mother?"

Cass just shrugged.

"You know your mother's probably not the best source for what's happening here at Forgotten Lake. She's sorta biased against the place."

"So ... Ham hasn't gotten a little bit scary?"

"Nah," Jack shook his head. "Oh, I suppose he's kinda nuts, but he's pretty much alone here at the lake, so he's not likely to cause any trouble. Only people he sees are me and Dup, and we just ignore him when he gets all goofy."

Cass chuckled. "Seems an ignominious end to the proud Madison lineage."

Jack scooped more fish from the oil and said, "Not exactly sure what an ignominious end is, but it sounds about right for Hamilton Madison."

* * *

Cass popped the last bite of walleye into her mouth and sat back with a happy sigh. The meal hadn't been fancy. It had consisted only of the fish, salad, and boiled potatoes with lots of butter and beer to wash it down. It was nothing like the pretentious fare at the French restaurant where she had dined the night before with her mother and Gerald, but given a choice between the two, she'd take Jack Baird's walleye any day.

She drained the last of her beer and said, "Thank you, Dad. That was delicious."

Jack shrugged modestly. "Hard to go wrong with walleye." He contemplated his own beer for a moment, then said, "Speaking of your mother ..."

"I didn't know we were."

"Well, you brought her up before."

"Actually, Dad, it was you who brought her up."

"Whatever," he said, waving a dismissive hand. "Anyway, how's she doing?"

Cass hesitated. The conversation had suddenly turned awkward, as she realized that she preferred talking about fish. "She seems ... happy enough."

"And she's moved in with this Gerald fella?"

"So it seems."

"What's he like, anyway?"

"Nice enough, I guess. He seems to have a lotta money." She paused. "How do *you* feel about all this? Does it bother you?"

Jack shrugged. "I'm getting used to it. And it's probably for the best. Your mother never liked it here at the lake. She hated it, actually, and that sorta poisoned everything else."

"And you're okay with living here all by yourself?"

He smiled. "Reckon I get a little grumpier every year, and that sorta suits me for living alone. There's just Dup and Ham, and that's about all the company I need, and most days I get along fine without them. Luckily, there's an island between here and their cabins, so most of the time it's like they're not even here."

"Mother said something about a dam—that you've been tangling with the county and the state over it."

Jack chuckled. "That's no big thing. Mostly, I've just been having fun with 'em, though truth be told, the lake could use a dam. It's too damn low and that's been raising hell with my boat."

They fell silent then, a comfortable silence, as Cass mused about her father doing battle with the local officialdom. That was nothing new. He had always done that, so it felt like old times. What had changed was that her mother was no longer there, and Cass was surprised at how little that bothered her. Despite Diane Baird's absence, Forgotten Lake still felt like home.

CHAPTER 6

*H*amilton Madison saw life as a series of trade-offs. In order to have something he badly wanted, he generally had to give something up to get it. His life on Forgotten Lake was surely that way, and for the most part that wasn't a problem. The things he had to give up weren't that highly valued, while the things he kept were.

Privacy was very high on Ham's value list, and if Forgotten Lake gave him nothing else, it gave him privacy. Jack Baird's big house was across the lake, but the island nicely blocked it from view. The only other person on the lake was Dup Dingle, and his cabin was two hundred yards up the shore and completely hidden by the surrounding woods, so Ham could sit in front of his cabin without having to acknowledge the presence of another soul. That was good. And the cost of that degree of privacy was being disconnected from the wider world, and since that meant being disconnected from the likes of Wall Street and Washington, it was hardly a cost at all. Wall Street was about greed, and only greed, and Ham despised it, but he despised Washington even more. Wall Street at least didn't mask its desire to get in everyone's pocket, but Washington was more insidious with its covert snooping into people's lives and, worse, its conspiring to take away the guns of true patriots.

Hamilton Madison thought himself a true patriot, and what's more, he believed himself to be a direct descendant of one of the truest patriots of all: James Madison, a chief architect of the U.S.

Constitution and the fourth president of the United States. It was one thing to be a patriot, but being a patriot with the added burden of the Madison family honor was quite something more, and Ham shouldered that burden gladly and with pride, and he took defense of the Constitution to be a sacred trust.

The world was full of scoffers, and at times some of them had questioned Ham's genealogical claims. Ham's usual response was to simply state that his father, Earl Madison, had told him so, and a father doesn't lie to his son. That, of course, didn't satisfy the more skeptical scoffers, so Ham had once undertaken to research and document his genealogy and settle the question once and for all. He started with every expectation that his studies would lead directly to Virginia and the Madison plantation, but after going back only a few generations, he found that the family line unexpectedly veered westward to South Dakota where his great-grandfather Amos experienced some difficulties with the law. Seems that Amos was a distiller of fine spirits, but his distrust of government—an apparent family trait—led him to withhold the taxes due on those spirits, and that led to jail time on two different occasions. That knowledge reassured Ham that he came from stalwart stock with the courage to fight government abuse, and while he was certain that researching additional generations would eventually lead back to Virginia, he chose to end his studies with Amos. After all, if a man couldn't believe his own father, then who could he believe?

There was one other issue where Ham opted for his father's version over another, and that was on the question of how he came to be named Hamilton. Now Earl Madison was generally regarded as an able promoter and salesman. Those of a more cynical view thought him a hustler and a conman, but everyone agreed that he had a gift of gab, especially when fortified by a shot or two of bourbon. Earl was so fortified on the day he put his hand on his son's shoulder, looked him in the eye, and said, "You're named for two great Americans, son, and I know that someday you'll be a great American too." Earl went on to relate how Alexander Hamilton and James Madison had joined together as the principal authors of the

Federalist Papers and were among the most ardent supporters of the Constitution. "And now, son, their names are joined together again in you, so do me and them proud."

That was Earl's version. The competing version went like this: It was the day of Ham's birth and Earl Madison was keeping the expectant father's vigil in the hospital waiting room. He was joined by another expectant father and the two of them commiserated and chain-smoked and shared an occasional nip from the pint bottle of bourbon in Earl's coat pocket. As the hours dragged on, boredom set in, and Earl, looking for ways to pass the time, produced a deck of cards from another coat pocket. Despite being a hustler and a conman, Earl was an imprudent gambler, and in short order he was down four dollars at gin rummy. Earl hated losing, and when the talk turned to speculation over the sex of their soon-to-be-born offspring, he saw a chance to recoup his losses.

"Boy or girl? Whaddaya think I'm gonna get?"

The other fellow shrugged. "It's fifty-fifty any way you look at."

It may have been fifty-fifty, but Earl had a hunch, and he always went with his hunches. Besides, he had been privy to the ultrasound, a new test their doctor had just started using. "I got ten bucks says it's a boy."

The other fellow, having never heard of an ultrasound, took the bet, and half an hour later when news came from the delivery room that Earl had a son, he handed over a ten-dollar bill. "So have you picked out a name yet?" the fellow asked.

Earl looked at the face on the ten spot he'd just won and smiled and said, "Gonna call the little fucker Hamilton."

That was the competing version as told to Ham by his mother, a version Ham chose to ignore. For one thing, his mother hadn't been there; she was in the recovery room. For another, she didn't like Earl much—they eventually divorced—and while bourbon might have been involved in Earl's version, his mother's fondness for gin fogged her own memory at times. And finally, it was just more seemly to claim that he'd been named for one of the authors of the Federalist Papers rather than as a result of a ten-dollar bet.

Ham had once even tried reading the Federalist Papers—it seemed the thing to do, as they'd been written by his ancestor and his namesake—but he found them so dry that he quit after a few pages. He still took his duty to the Constitution seriously, but he preferred the writing of present-day true patriots, and that led to another trade-off. One advantage to his life on Forgotten Lake was that it minimized the risk of electronic snooping by the government. There was no reliable cellular service and Ham had no landline, so there were no phone calls to be tracked or tapped into. Nor was cable available, but Ham did sign up for satellite TV, as it provided Internet access, which was his only exposure to the electronic snoops. It was indeed a trade-off, but he willingly took the chance, as it connected him to his network of true patriots. Oh, there were true patriots nearby in Minnesota, plenty of them, but to benefit from the full breadth of the movement, he had to be in touch with patriots in places like Idaho and Texas, places where they took their patriotism seriously. And being connected coast to coast was essential for the patriots to win the day when the Big Showdown with the government came, as it surely would.

On this evening, like most evenings, Hamilton Madison sat in an Adirondack chair in front of his cabin, watching the sun set over the island and sipping bourbon on the rocks—a taste acquired from his father. He was nearly fifty years old and his hair was turning gray—steely gray, he liked to think—and he wore his usual attire: camo pants and shirt, the garb of true patriots. If Hamilton and Madison were alive today, they would surely wear camo too, just as they would surely join Ham's cause to fight the desecration of the Constitution they labored so lovingly to create. Vigilance, that was the key. The true patriots had to be ready for the Big Showdown, just as the minutemen had been ready at Lexington and Concord, and that meant avoiding distractions.

Now as Ham sipped his bourbon, he nodded ruefully at a distraction right there on Forgotten Lake: Jack Baird's silly ongoing battle over his dam. Ham liked Jack, but sadly Jack had become a doddering old fool, and his dam was the sort of minor skirmish that served only to divert attention away from the government's evil plans, and those plans didn't involve dams and lakes—they involved guns. Well, the government would never take Hamilton Madison's guns, his collection of rifles and shotguns and handguns, all twelve of them, because he avoided distractions and kept his powder dry as he awaited the Big Showdown when true patriots across the land would rise up to save the Constitution.

CHAPTER 7

*C*ass Baird made her way from the house down to the dock wearing only a swimsuit and flip-flops with a towel slung over her shoulder. It had been a long time, too long, since she had swum in Forgotten Lake and on this morning, her first morning back, the lake beckoned irresistibly. She stood at the end of the dock savoring the scene: clear sky, blue water, a light breeze rippling the surface, vivid green of birch and pine across the way on the island, a loon calling in the distance. Perfect, absolutely perfect. It was nearly ten o'clock and she felt the sun's warmth on her bare skin, but she knew better than to let that warmth deceive her. Even in late summer Forgotten Lake would be cool, not June cold, but still cool enough to shock the sleepiest skin awake. Sleepy skin? Cass wasn't sure she had the right metaphor, but she did know that a dive into this water promised refreshing delight to every pore. She dropped the towel and slipped out of her flip-flops and stood poised to dive, her toes curled around the dock's edge, but then she hesitated. Her father was gone. He and Dup Dingle had taken a pickup load of firewood to town and wouldn't be back for several hours. There wasn't another soul to be seen anywhere, which was normal for Forgotten Lake, and it suddenly seemed a grand idea to swim naked, as she often had as a young girl. If the cool water refreshed the skin, why deny any pore? She peeled off her suit and stood at naked attention for a long moment; then she dove in.

It was just as she remembered: a fine line between shock and ecstasy, a chilling pleasure to every square inch of skin as she knifed through the water. She surfaced twenty feet from the dock where she treaded water for nearly a minute as she adjusted to the coolness before breaking into a crawl. She was a strong swimmer—she'd grown up on a lake, after all—and she swam smoothly and effortlessly all the way to the island. There she climbed onto a large rock at the shore where she sat savoring the sun's warmth after the lake's chill. It was the same rock she had often perched naked on as a young girl, the same rock where she had imagined herself the little mermaid in Copenhagen's harbor.

She basked there for a time, delighting in the mix of memory and sun warmth and pine-scented air, before reluctantly climbing down and swimming back across the lake. She pulled herself onto the dock, patted away the beads of water on her body with the towel, and started to put on her swimsuit but then thought better of it. Why bother tugging on a suit over damp skin when it felt so good to be naked? She slipped into her flip-flops and tossed the towel over her shoulder; then with swimsuit in hand, she made her way up the path. At the house she crossed the deck and was reaching for the French doors leading into the great room when she was startled by a sound. She turned just as a man came round the corner of the house ten feet away. Cass froze. The man froze. Then the man said, "Oops!"

* * *

"I'm ... I'm so sorry for barging in like that," Brian Walsh said for the second time. He and Cass were now seated at the table on the deck. She wore a blue terry cloth robe and she couldn't help being a little amused at his level of embarrassment. Immediately following their surprise encounter, she had quickly wrapped the towel around her and had begun backing toward the French doors while he muttered apologies and something about county business. He, too, was backing away, on the verge of fleeing, when suddenly she didn't want the encounter to end without the chance for explanation: his explanation of why he was there and hers of why she had been prancing around naked.

"Give me a minute," she had said. "I'll get a robe and we can start over."

Now, sitting across the table from each other, he was still having trouble with eye contact, and that added to her amusement and her sense that this man posed no threat.

"I ... I came to see Jack," he explained.

"I assumed as much."

"I didn't expect anyone else to be here. I thought Jack lived alone."

"I'm visiting."

"Oh."

"I'm his daughter. Cass Baird."

"Oh." He risked eye contact. "I'm Brian Walsh with the Soil and Water Conservation District."

"Yeah, you said that already." She smiled. "Look, this is obviously an embarrassing situation, but it's my fault. You were just going about your business. I'm the one who was walking around in the buff in broad daylight. By the way, I don't normally do that."

"I shouldn't have just shown up like that," he said. "I should've called ahead."

"Wouldn't have made any difference because I was swimming. I'd just gotten out of the lake when you arrived."

"Yeah, I sorta figured that out. Your hair's wet." He managed to hold her gaze for a moment; then he broke into a sheepish grin. "And I'm sorry to keep apologizing, but it's ... well, pretty awkward."

"I know what you mean. It's always awkward when this happens. Why, just the other day I scared away a Jehovah's Witness."

His grin turned to surprise and Cass realized that he wasn't any more ready for her sense of humor than he had been for her nakedness. "Just kidding," she said; then she took a moment to study him more closely. He seemed about her age. He wore jeans and a flannel shirt and hiking boots, and he looked as if he'd be comfortable in the woods. He wasn't Hollywood handsome, and that was fine with Cass—most men who were, usually were insufferable—but she found Brian Walsh attractive in an unpretentious, comfortable way. Anyhow, it was time to turn the conversation to business. "My dad'll be back in a couple hours. Can I give him a message?"

He thought for a moment. "Maybe I should come back later. I'd really like to talk to him." A pause. "It's about his dam."

"Ah, the infamous Jack Baird dam that now threatens life as we know it in the North Country."

A wary look now, then Brian said, "If by that you mean this thing is getting blown out of proportion, then I tend to agree, but that won't change the fact that a county commissioner, who also happens to be an affected property owner, sees it differently."

"So you're saying my dad's dam has become political?"

"Unfortunately, yes."

"Then what do you hope to accomplish by talking to him?"

He shrugged. "Not sure. I guess I'm hoping to work out some sort of compromise. Maybe get Jack to take the dam down temporarily while he applies to get it permitted."

"What are his chances of getting a permit?"

Another shrug. "Under the circumstances, I'd say less than fifty percent."

"So you want my dad to accept a bad compromise just to make life easier for you?"

A pained expression now. "Look, it might be better if I wait and talk to Jack about this."

"Actually, I'm authorized to act as his attorney in this matter." This was a lie, and Cass had no idea why she had said it, other than feeling a sudden desire to inject herself into the great Forgotten Lake dam controversy. Or maybe she just wanted to continue her conversation with Brian Walsh?

"Are ... are you an attorney?"

She shook her head. "I'm an economist."

Surprise registered on Brian's face. "I never would've guessed that."

"That's because you've probably never seen a naked one before."

He stared for a moment, his mouth slightly open; then he put his head back and laughed, and when he looked at her again, it seemed to Cass that the tension between them had eased. "Well, attorney or not, I think it's best that I come back later and talk directly to Jack, though if you want to sit in, Ms. Baird, I'd have no problem."

"Call me Cass. Or if you want to keep it formal, then it's Dr. Baird."

"I'll opt for Cass." He smiled. "And I'm beginning to wish we had met under different circumstances."

She shrugged. "Circumstances can change."

CHAPTER 8

*D*riving his pickup back from town, Jack Baird glanced over at Dup Dingle who was nodding off in the passenger seat. Jack smiled, thinking that Dup had certainly earned his rest that day. Earlier Jack had sipped coffee from his thermos and looked on while Dup heaped the pickup box high with birch firewood. Later Jack had stood by with Henry Goltz, watching and drinking beer as Dup unloaded the wood and stacked it at the side of Henry's General Store.

Henry's General Store sold gas and groceries and beer and bait and, as of that day anyway, firewood. If you needed something that Henry didn't sell, it involved another thirty minutes of driving, as he was pretty much the only show in town. For that matter, calling the area a town was quite a stretch. In addition to the general store there were only six modest houses, most of them needing paint, also a bar and a church. The church had closed a dozen years earlier, but the bar managed to hang on, which Jack took as commentary on the local spiritual needs. Early residents had hoped the town would one day be incorporated into a municipality under the name of Grandview. Sadly, incorporation never happened, and eventually everyone gave up on any lingering notions of grandness, and now they just called the place Clyde's Corner. Clyde was Henry's father and the general store's original owner. When Clyde died, there was talk of changing the hamlet's name to Henry's Corner to reflect the store's new ownership, but that was overruled as playing fast and loose with tradition, to the extent that Clyde's Corner enjoyed any tradition. Besides, everyone rather liked the alliterative sound of Clyde's Corner.

As promised, Henry paid Dup $120 for the wood, and then Dup paid the $20 he had promised to Jack. Most of the remaining hundred dollars was now back in Henry's possession, as Dup had stocked up on needed supplies. The pickup box, now empty of firewood, carried four cases of beer and a case of Little Debbie French Rolls, and those supplies, Jack understood, were a source of true contentment to Dup. Dup's sleep, therefore, wasn't just the rest of a weary man. It was the sleep of a man freed from want and worry. For now, anyway, Dup had everything he needed. There'd be no hotel room at the Duluth Radisson, there'd be no hooker, but Dup was going home to his humble cabin on Forgotten Lake with a good supply of beer and snack cakes. Really, what more could a man want? And if he had other needs, there was always his moss box.

Rounding the south end of the lake on their way to Dup's cabin, they came to the bridge over the Bumble River and Jack pulled to the side of the road and stopped.

Dup blinked awake and looked around. "What's up?"

"Gonna check my dam," Jack said.

Jack and Dup made their way along the path that followed the Bumble through a hundred yards of woods to the lakeshore. There they found the water on the dam's lakeside up to within an inch of the top while on the downstream side the river was reduced to a trickle.

Dup whistled. "Goddamn, Jack, she's about up to the top."

Jack nodded. "That's right where it oughta be." He then pointed to the trickle and chuckled. "Don't suppose that asshole downstream's any too happy though."

"Don't suppose," Dup agreed. "Who is he, anyway?"

"They never said, and that kinda pisses me off. Seems like if a fella tries to tell another fella what to do with his property, then the first fella oughta have enough balls to say so himself 'stead of hiding out behind a bunch of bureaucrats."

Dup shook his head. "Ain't right."

"No it ain't, but there's no point in worrying about it, 'cause the county boys'll be along any day now to take it out again."

"What'll you do then?"

Jack shrugged, then grinned. "Reckon I'll just have to put her in again."

CHAPTER 9

$\mathscr{B}$rian Walsh stared glumly at the clutter on his desk and tried to concentrate, but concentration wasn't coming easily that morning. Each time he tried to focus on a particular task, he was soon distracted by the image of a certain naked economist who kept slipping into his thoughts. Cass Baird had indeed dominated his thoughts since their embarrassing encounter on Jack Baird's deck the previous morning. It had lasted only a moment—she had quickly covered herself with a towel—but that moment was now burned into his memory. *You've been too long without a woman,* he told himself with a chuckle, but he knew it was more than that, more than just the lovely sight of Cass's body. It was the way she had so gracefully handled an awkward situation, even managing to inject some humor, that now intrigued him every bit as much as the memory of her bare breasts. He wished they had met under different circumstances. If he were to approach her now, if he were to ask her out, the awkwardness of their first meeting would hang over them like a cloud. Still, circumstances can change. Those had been Cass's exact words, circumstances can change, and Brian now found himself imagining ways to make that happen.

"Walsh!"

Brian was jolted from his reverie as Zack Buchwald, the office manager, came round the corner barking his name. Brian sat up. He was accustomed to Zack's habit of making mountains of molehills, but any hope of easily dealing with Zack's perceived crisis that day was quickly dashed as County Commissioner Dugan came into view behind Zack.

In Brian's work, first as a consulting engineer in Minneapolis and now with the Soil and Water Conservation District, he was used to dealing with local elected officials. Some were easy to work with, some weren't, and in Brian's view county commissioners stood out from the others as being the most likely to devolve into despotic bullies.

Roscoe P. Dugan fit that description perfectly. He had been a commissioner for over twelve years and any sense of humility he might have once brought to his office was now squashed beneath the weight of his insufferable self-importance. Brian found it ironic that Dugan's actual physical presence was such a complete mismatch for his delusions of grandeur. He was short and bald with a dumpling body, and he was cursed with a prodigious capacity to sweat. Sweat readily beaded on his bald scalp and stained the armpits of his shirt, even in the dead of winter. In warm weather, sweat dripped regularly from the tip of his nose. This combined to comical effect with his tendency to respond to any challenge to his thinking by saying, "No sweat." It was never a good day when Dugan found reason to visit the Soil and Water Conservation office, and today Brian feared the subject would be the Rumble on the Bumble.

"When's that dam coming out?" Zack demanded, getting right to the point and confirming Brian's premonition.

It wasn't a topic Brian was happy to discuss, but at least he had a ready answer. "Today. This morning. Perhaps as we speak."

"More to the point," Zack said, "we need to talk about what you're gonna do to make sure Baird doesn't put it in again."

What I'm going to do? Brian thought, wondering how the dam had become his sole responsibility, but in the interest of discretion he didn't ask.

"This dog and pony show's gotta stop," Commissioner Dugan spoke up now. "It's getting ridiculous. He puts it in, we take it out; he puts it in, we take it out. It's ... it's fucking absurd!"

Despite himself, Brian chuckled and nodded. "Yeah, it's getting to be a bit like the Myth of Sisyphus." He immediately regretted saying that, though, as Zack and Dugan both gaped with blank stares.

"The myth of what?" Dugan asked.

"Sisyphus." Brian shrugged. "Sisyphus was an ancient Greek who was condemned by the gods to roll a big rock up a hill for all eternity. Only, whenever he got near the top, the rock would roll back down and he'd have to start over again. It's ... it's a metaphor for absurdity."

Zack rolled his eyes. Dugan shook his head and turned to Zack. "You see, that's the trouble with this goddamn office. You got people babbling about myths, for Chrissake. Forget the fucking myths already. Start dealing in reality."

Zack, clearly unhappy at being linked to staff folly, attempted to redirect Dugan's fury. "Read this," he said, thrusting a letter at Brian.

Brian got no further than the letterhead, which identified the local district court, before Dugan interrupted. "That's from Judge Larson to Baird. Says that if Baird puts the dam in again, he'll be in contempt of court and his ass'll wind up in jail. And that's a fucking guarantee."

Brian quickly scanned the letter, saw that it did indeed threaten jail, though in language less coarse than Dugan's. "So why are you giving this to me?"

His question had been directed to Zack but Dugan answered. "Because you're gonna go out to Baird's today and hand-deliver that letter and make goddamn sure he understands what's gonna happen if he puts it in again."

"Why me?" Brian asked. "Seems like the sheriff's people oughta handle something like this."

"You're gonna do it because I say you're gonna do it," Dugan said. "You're the one who let this whole goddamn thing get outta hand in the first place. So now you're gonna deal with it."

"Jack Baird can be pretty stubborn," Brian said. "I could see him defying this, and then we'll be stuck with the negative publicity from throwing an eighty-year-old guy in jail just for trying to improve his property."

Dugan waved his hand dismissively. "No sweat. Baird may be stupid, but he ain't that stupid." He pulled out a handkerchief and mopped sweat from his brow. "One more thing, Walsh. I want you to call me after you've delivered that letter. I wanna make damn sure he knows what the picture is, and I want him to know it today." Dugan mopped more sweat and turned to leave; then he turned back. "And one last thing, I don't wanna hear any more coming outta this office about metaphors or the myth of syphilis or any of that crap. Try sticking to reality."

* * *

Brian sat staring glumly at Judge Larson's letter. It angered him that he'd been singled out to deal with Jack Baird's dam. It was a legal matter. The sheriff's people should handle it. He looked at his watch. Ten-thirty. Deputy Sam Skinner and the county boys probably had the dam out by now and were sitting down to coffee and doughnuts with Jack Baird. All very civil, all very cordial, and next would come Brian Walsh with threats from the judge. He shook his head. He had hoped for different circumstances with Cass, but threatening her father with jail time didn't seem the sort of new circumstances likely to generate warm feelings. Maybe Dugan was right, after all. Maybe the metaphor that best described this situation really was the myth of syphilis.

CHAPTER 10

*A*s often happens, a seemingly unrelated incident can unleash an unfortunate chain of events. That was the case the day that the Rumble on the Bumble took a sudden and decided turn for the worse, the unrelated incident in question being a toothache that Deputy Sam Skinner woke with the morning before. By noon the pain had increased to the point that he sought relief from his dentist, who informed the deputy that he needed a root canal, and an appointment was made for the next morning with a specialist in Duluth. By two o'clock in the afternoon Deputy Skinner was back at the sheriff's office where he remembered that he was scheduled to oversee the removal of Jack Baird's dam on Forgotten Lake the following morning. Sam wasn't one to shirk duty, and he was also looking forward to the coffee and doughnuts by the lake that had become part of the dam removal protocol, so he asked if the removal might be delayed one day.

"Not a chance," said Hank Cross, the supervising deputy at the sheriff's office in Forsythe. "Roscoe Dugan's raising all kinds of hell over this, so it's gotta get done like right now. Dilworth can do it."

Deputy Carter Dilworth was twenty-two years old and the newest man in the department. He was also, in the opinion of Deputy Carter Dilworth, the most squared-away officer on the force. His uniform was always spotless, the creases on his shirt and trousers sharp, his shoes shined, his face steely and impassive behind aviator shades, his posture ramrod straight. And Deputy Dilworth always went by the book. As he saw it, the law was meant to be followed, not interpreted or subjected to the mushy empathy exhibited by some of the other deputies. The psychological profile that had been part of Dilworth's hiring process described him as being "guided by strict linear thinking that will serve him well in clearly defined situations that do not require extensive discernment or subjective judgment." In less clinical terms, Sam Skinner had described Dilworth as an uptight prick who couldn't find his own ass in a snowstorm, but he agreed with Cross that Dilworth might be up to overseeing the removal of Jack Baird's dam. He would, however, regret missing out on the coffee and doughnuts by the lake.

* * *

Jack Baird's day had started well. It was a beautiful morning, and he had just enjoyed a breakfast of scrambled eggs and bacon with Cass at the table out on the deck. Now they sat back, basking in the warm sun and sipping coffee, as they contemplated the day ahead. Jack nodded toward the lake where a light breeze rippled the surface. "Maybe we oughta take the boat out and see if we can't hook a walleye or two."

Cass nodded. "Sounds perfect, but I'd like to take a walk in the woods first, just a half hour or so to stretch my legs."

"Go for it," Jack said. "While you're doing that, I'll tie a new hook and sinker on your old rod; then we can head out as soon as you get back."

They cleared away the breakfast dishes and Cass took off for her walk and Jack went about getting the gear ready for their fishing trip. He was in a fine mood and much of that had to do with his daughter being there. He had grown quite comfortable with living alone, and he doubted that he could share his life with just anyone again, but Cass was different. Cass loved Forgotten Lake as much as he did. She knew how to be happy there, and now he relished the thought of spending a day with her on the water. He got Cass's rod ready; then he carried the two rods along with his tackle box and landing net down to the dock and loaded it all into the boat. His minnow bucket was tied off to the dock and he pulled it from the water, checked to see that the minnows were still swimming, and loaded that into the boat too. He then surveyed the gear to make sure they had everything they would need, and he had just decided to go back to the house for an iced-down six-pack of beer when Dup Dingle puttered up in his boat, bumping to a stop against the dock.

Jack was in no mood to share his daughter with anyone that day, certainly not Dup Dingle, and he snarled, "What the hell you want?"

Dup squinted up at Jack from his boat. "What got you so owly today?"

"I ain't owly. I'm about to go fishing with Cass, so whatever you got in mind, I ain't got time for it."

Dup shrugged. "Suit yourself. I just figured you'd wanna know that the county boys are down at the south end a the lake taking out your dam."

"What?"

"I was just now passing by in my boat and there they were, busy as a bunch a beavers."

"Goddamn it!" Jack was seized by sudden anger. This wasn't right. Sam Skinner always stopped by the house first. How else was Jack to know to bring coffee and doughnuts? There had been an understanding of how things were to be. It had been gentlemanly and civil, and now the county had gone and screwed it all up. Well Jack Baird wasn't going to stand for it. He looked at his watch. Cass wouldn't be back for fifteen minutes or so, but he didn't want to wait until then. In fifteen minutes he could get to the dam, raise hell with the county, and be back in time to go fishing. He turned to Dup. "Run me down there, will ya?"

"Sure, Jack, hop in."

Jack started to step into Dup's boat; then he hesitated. Just raising hell didn't feel like enough of a response. The county was screwing with him. They were the ones who'd raised the ante, and now Jack felt a need to raise it back in a way that would get their attention.

"Wait here," he said to Dup, and then strode up the dock to the house. A minute later he returned, carrying a 12-gauge shotgun.

"Whoa there, Jack," Dup said. "What the hell you think you're gonna do with that?"

"Make a statement," Jack said, climbing into the boat.

"That's a pretty bad idea, Jack. I mean, you really don't wanna go shooting anybody."

"I ain't gonna shoot anyone. It ain't even loaded."

"Then why bring it?"

"To make them understand that I'm seriously pissed."

"But the county boys won't know your gun ain't loaded. They'll assume—"

"You gonna take me down there or not?" Jack glared at Dup.

Dup hesitated a moment longer; then he pulled the starter cord.

* * *

Deputy Carter Dilworth was annoyed. He was supposed to be investigating the break-in of a convenience store, a task worthy of his sleuthing skills, but at the last minute Supervising Deputy Hank Cross had assigned him to oversee a county work detail charged with removing a stupid dam on Forgotten Lake. It was a task clearly unworthy of Deputy Dilworth's talents, and making matters worse, he'd had to tramp through a hundred yards of woods to get to the site, and now his well-shined shoes were scuffed and his trouser creases were wilting. And if all that wasn't enough, there was the final indignity: the county work detail itself. There were two of them, a slovenly pair with shirttails hanging out and several days of beard stubble—shoddy appearances that proved to be a good indicator of their work ethic. They had no sooner arrived on site than they started whining because Dilworth hadn't notified the property owner. Sam Skinner always did, they said, and then the owner would come around with coffee and doughnuts.

Dilworth could scarcely believe his ears. *Coffee and doughnuts?* He knew the highway department was a lax bunch, but Sam Skinner was a deputy. He was supposed to be squared away and go by the book. Well, that sort of thing wasn't going to happen on Deputy Carter Dilworth's watch. "This is not a coffee party, gentlemen," he informed the work detail in a steely tone. "We are executing a court order and we will do so in a professional and disciplined manner."

The workers didn't receive Deputy Dilworth's leadership cheerfully, though they had no choice but to accept it. Now Dilworth nodded with satisfaction as the dam had been removed and the Bumble River was once more flowing freely. The men were gathering up their gear and preparing to leave when the sound of an approaching motorboat caused all heads to turn.

There were two men in the boat. It came straight in and skidded onto the sandy beach. The man sitting forward quickly climbed out and headed straight for the deputy and the workers. Deputy Dilworth instinctively sensed trouble and he focused all his faculties to assess the threat. The man had white hair and appeared to be elderly, which wasn't threatening, but he also seemed very agitated and was in fact cursing. Deputy Dilworth's eyes then widened behind his aviator shades with the realization that the man was wielding a firearm, what appeared to be a 12-gauge shotgun. Now that was a threat! Deputy Dilworth then acted with what he would later describe as the prompt and appropriate response of a trained law enforcement professional in the face of a terrorist attack. In short, he drew his gun, aimed at the charging terrorist, and fired a shot.

The shot missed. The terrorist stopped dead in his tracks, a stunned look on his face, and said, "What the fuck!"

Deputy Dilworth understood that a threat still existed. The terrorist still had a gun, though it was now pointed at the ground, and he still appeared to be belligerent. "Drop the gun," the deputy ordered.

"What the hell did you shoot at me for?"

"Drop it!"

"Aw, hell, sonny, it ain't even—"

"Drop the gun!" repeated Deputy Dilworth. "Now!"

The terrorist shook his head and dropped the gun.

Deputy Dilworth took a menacing step forward, his gun aimed at the terrorist's chest. "Facedown on the ground."

"Now, look—"

"On the ground!"

Still shaking his head, the terrorist slowly lowered himself to the ground, and only then did Deputy Dilworth holster his gun, pull handcuffs from his belt, and snap them on the man's wrists behind his back.

One of the county workers walked up to where the deputy now stood over the terrorist. "That there's Jack Baird you just put them cuffs on. He owns this here land, and if you woulda told him we were coming, he probably woulda come round with coffee and doughnuts, 'steada that there shotgun."

Deputy Dilworth turned angrily to the man. "This was a terrorist attack, and now it's a crime scene, so you just back off and let me handle things."

"Jack didn't mean no harm by it. He was just pissed is all."

This came from behind the deputy and he whirled to find the second man from the boat, a likely accomplice, walking toward him. The deputy's hand went to his gun again, though he didn't draw it, as the accomplice appeared to be unarmed. Still, the deputy eyed him carefully. The man, while not presenting an immediate threat, looked unsavory, and Deputy Dilworth took that as a warning sign. "Who are you?" he demanded.

"Dup Dingle. And Jack didn't do nothing illegal. Hell, he owns this land."

"I'll decide what's legal and what isn't." Deputy Dilworth then briefly pondered the situation before making his professional judgment. "In fact, you're both under arrest."

Dup Dingle stared in disbelief and the terrorist on the ground looked up and said, "What the fuck for?"

Deputy Dilworth ignored the question and coolly gave both men their Miranda warning.

* * *

And so the Rumble on the Bumble escalated from a somewhat congenial spat between a property owner and local government to a nasty confrontation resulting in arrests. It was still, however, a minor incident between a hotheaded old man and an overzealous young cop. There was every expectation that cooler heads would soon prevail, and that might well have occurred, but for what happened next.

The county work detail led the way from the lake through the woods to the road where their truck was parked next to the deputy's cruiser. Right behind them came Deputy Dilworth and the two men he had just taken into custody. Just as they all reached the road, a pickup drove up, slowed, and came to a stop. From behind the wheel Hamilton Madison rolled down his window and gaped in wonder as the deputy opened the cruiser's trunk and placed the shotgun he was carrying inside. Jack Baird stood next to the cruiser, his hands cuffed behind his back, and the deputy then pushed Jack's head down, directing him into the backseat. Dup Dingle stood passively waiting for Jack to slide across the seat so that he, too, could climb in.

"Hey, Dup," Ham called out. "What the hell's going on?"

"Me and Jack just got arrested," Dup said, "and they took Jack's gun away."

With that the deputy pushed Dup into the cruiser, and moments later the county truck and the cruiser drove off down the road, leaving behind an astonished Hamilton Madison. Ham's astonishment then quickly turned into a seething rage as Dup's parting words seared into his brain. "They took Jack's gun away!" The government had come onto a man's property and taken the man's gun. This was it. This was the Big Showdown. It was time for true patriots everywhere to heed the call to action.

CHAPTER 11

*B*rian Walsh arrived at Jack Baird's place with mixed emotions. For the entire thirty-minute drive from his office in Forsythe to Forgotten Lake he had wavered between dread and hope—dreading the reaction to the letter he carried from Judge Larson, yet hoping that Jack, and more importantly Cass, wouldn't shoot the messenger. He parked next to Jack's pickup and the car he assumed to be Cass's, climbed from his pickup, and made his way to the lake side of the house.

Just as he rounded the corner and stepped onto the deck, he came face-to-face with Cass. It was the second time in barely twenty-four hours that they had met unexpectedly on that deck, though this time under markedly different circumstances. He summoned what he hoped was a winsome smile and blurted, "You're all dressed!"

His comment had been an attempt at humor, a rather lame one that he immediately regretted, as Cass glared at him with narrowed eyes that showed no trace of amusement. She spoke in an icy tone. "What do you want?"

"Um ... is Jack here?"

"No, he's not." More ice.

"Oh ... well, I'm supposed to ... I was ordered to give him this." He held out the judge's letter.

Cass took the letter and quickly scanned it; then to Brian's surprise she laughed, a cold, humorless laugh. "How thoughtful of you

50

to drive all the way out here and deliver this warning," she said, her voice dripping with sarcasm. "But I'm afraid it's a little late."

He gave her a questioning look. "Meaning?"

"Meaning I just got a call from Dad. He's been arrested. He's in jail in Forsythe."

"Arrested for what?"

Cass shrugged. "I'm not sure. He wasn't making a lot of sense over the phone. Something to do with this stupid dam business."

Brian shook his head in disbelief. "Okay, Sam Skinner was supposed to bring a county crew out here today to take the dam out, but I can't imagine Sam letting things get outta hand like that. He's already taken the dam out a couple times, and nothing like this has ever happened. Hell, they usually have coffee and doughnuts with your dad."

"Who's Sam Skinner?"

"A sheriff's deputy. He kinda likes your dad, and he's halfway sympathetic about the dam. This just doesn't make any sense."

"Well, making sense or not, it's happened," she said, "and now I'm on my way into Forsythe to see about bailing him out or getting an attorney or whatever needs to be done."

"I'll follow you in."

"That's not necessary."

"Yeah, it is," he said. "Like it or not, I've been involved in this mess from the start, and now I need to find out what happened."

* * *

The jail in Forsythe wasn't a real jail, just two temporary holding cells at the back of the sheriff's office. Both cells were presently occupied, one by Jack Baird, the other by Dup Dingle. Hank Cross, the supervising deputy in Forsythe, sat glumly in his office near the front of the building. Earlier in the day he had entertained hopes of sneaking away early and going fishing. Those hopes were now dashed, and worse, he was faced with an administrative hornet's nest that was likely to complicate his life for days to come, a mess he blamed on the man seated across the desk from him.

Cross now repeated what he'd just been told, as if he couldn't quite believe it. "You actually discharged your weapon? You shot your goddamn gun?"

Deputy Carter Dilworth thrust his chin out defiantly. "He charged me with a shotgun. What was I supposed to do?" After a moment's thought, he added, "Besides, it was my duty to protect the county workers."

Cross snorted. "But Baird didn't fire his gun, right?"

"Correct."

"Did he aim it at you?"

Dilworth hesitated. "Sort of."

"Sort of? What the hell's that supposed to mean? He either did or he didn't."

"He was waving it around like a madman, Hank. And he was shouting incoherently. I only had a split second to react, and as far as I'm concerned I went strictly by the book."

Cross slumped wearily back in his chair. "What kind of load did he have in the shotgun?"

"Um ..." Dilworth suddenly looked less defiant. "It wasn't loaded."

Cross bolted upright, gaping in disbelief. "Not loaded?"

"Correct. But I had no way of knowing that."

"Aw, Jesus H. Christ!" Cross slumped back again, and after a moment he said, "Okay, so this is where we are: you arrested a man on his own property for carrying an unloaded gun."

"C'mon, Hank, that's not—"

"Shut up!" Cross paused to glare at Dilworth. "Now this is what's gonna happen next. There'll be no charges brought against either man. And they'll be released immediately with the hope that the whole goddamn mess just goes away."

"Not gonna happen."

This came from the open doorway of the office and Cross turned to see Roscoe "No Sweat" Dugan standing there. *Aw, crap,*

Cross thought, *and I didn't think things could get any worse.* "Look, Commissioner—" he started to say, but Dugan cut him off.

"Baird's a goddamn menace," Dugan said. "He belongs in jail. As a commissioner *and* as a citizen of this county, I demand that you hold him."

"Charged with what?" asked Cross.

Dugan was momentarily at a loss for words and he looked to Deputy Dilworth, who somewhat timidly suggested, "Terroristic threats?"

"That a felony?" Dugan asked.

Cross nodded.

"Works for me then," Dugan said. "Lock the bastards up and throw away the key."

Cross wearily shook his head. "Okay, I'll hold 'em for now, but I'm taking this to the sheriff and the county attorney down in Duluth. They'll decide what, if anything, they get charged with."

Dugan didn't look happy, but Cross knew the commissioner was less likely to meddle if the heavies from Duluth were involved. "Well, alright," Dugan said, "but shouldn't you have people out there at that lake gathering evidence?"

"Suppose you let me worry about that, Commissioner."

Dugan looked no happier. "There is a court order involved here, you know."

"Yeah," Cross nodded. "But that bars Baird from putting the dam in again. He hasn't done that."

"Not yet. You turn him loose and he sure as hell will."

Hank Cross eyed Dugan with thinly veiled contempt, noting with disgust the sweat-soaked armpits of his shirt. He'd had enough of the perspiring commissioner for one day. "We'll see what the sheriff and county attorney have to say."

Dugan glared at Cross for a long moment. "I might give the county attorney a call myself."

"Now, Commissioner, you wouldn't want to give the appearance of meddling in a legal proceeding, would you?"

Dugan offered a sneer. "No sweat, Deputy, no sweat."

* * *

Brian Walsh's drive back to Forsythe from Forgotten Lake was even more nerve racking than the drive out there had been. On the earlier trip he had worried about the reaction to the judge's letter. Those worries now paled to this latest turn of events: Jack Baird's arrest. What had gone wrong? He still couldn't imagine Sam Skinner letting things get so out of hand, but apparently things had gotten out of hand and Jack was in jail. Now, following Cass into town, he was having trouble keeping up with her, and he feared her ever-increasing speed to be a measure of ever-increasing anger.

To his relief, they avoided both speeding tickets and accidents and made it safely into Forsythe where Cass parked in front of the sheriff's office. Brian parked next to her and when he climbed from his pickup, she turned to him.

"You don't have to do this," she said, still an icy edge to her voice. "I think perhaps you've helped enough already."

"Yeah," he said, "I need to do this. In a way I feel responsible for what's happened. I know I look like one of the bad guys, but I really have been trying to help. It may not seem like it, but I *am* on Jack's side."

She eyed him skeptically for a long moment. "Alright, let's go find out what the jailbird did."

Just inside the front door in the anteroom of the sheriff's office, they met Deputy Sam Skinner. One side of his face was puffy and swollen, causing Brian to fear that assaulting a law officer was part of Jack's offense.

"What happened, Sam?" Brian asked.

Skinner shook his head. "Not sure. I'm still trying to get a handle on it."

"What do you mean, you're not sure? You were out there, weren't you?"

"No, I just got back from the dentist in Duluth." Skinner pointed to his swollen jaw. "Goddamn root canal. Hank sent Dilworth out with the work detail, and somehow things went bad."

"What's he charged with?" asked Cass.

Skinner turned to her. "Who are you?"

"This is Cass Baird," Brian volunteered. "Jack's daughter."

Skinner nodded. "Nice to meet you, ma'am." After a moment's reflection, he added, "Wish it was under better circumstances."

"Me too," Cass said. "So what is he charged with?"

"So far as I know, *they* aren't charged with anything yet."

"They?" asked Brian.

"Dilworth brought Dup Dingle in too."

"Aw, Jesus," Brian said. "So what happens next?"

Skinner shrugged and lowered his voice. "Just between us, I think Hank wants to release 'em and forget it ever happened, but Roscoe Dugan's raising hell about it, so Hank referred it to the sheriff and the county attorney down in Duluth."

"Well, when might we know something?" Cass asked.

As if on cue, a door opened off the anteroom and Hank Cross stepped out. He nodded to Brian, looked questioningly at Cass, and Skinner made introductions. Skinner then asked, "Any word from Duluth?"

"Yeah, I just got off the phone," Cross said. "The sheriff agrees with me that we should drop everything and release them, but the county attorney's not quite there. He said to release them without charges, but to hold onto Jack's shotgun while he studies the matter further."

"What's to study?" asked Cass.

Cross looked at her and shrugged. "Not much. I think it's mostly a matter of Roscoe Dugan bending his ear over the phone, so now the county attorney wants to look thorough. Which is a nice way of saying he's covering his ass. I expect Jack'll have his gun back in a few days; then we can just forget this ever happened." A pause. "So long as Jack doesn't put the dam in again. Then he *will* be in serious trouble."

"So I can take him home now?" Cass asked.

"It'll be about fifteen minutes," Cross said. "Paperwork, you know. But you can go back and see them. Sam'll show you the way."

* * *

The occupants of the two holding cells offered quite a contrast. In one, Dup Dingle sat on a bunk, staring glumly at the floor, shoulders sagging, looking small and defeated. In the other, Jack Baird paced angrily, and when Cass and Brian came in, he stopped and jabbed a finger at Brian. "What the hell's he doing here?"

"He's on our side, Dad," Cass said.

Brian was pleased to hear Cass say that, but Jack looked unconvinced. "Sure as hell coulda fooled me."

"We can talk about it later," said Cass. "So what happened out there anyway?"

"The son of a bitch shot at me, is what happened. He tried to kill me. And on my own goddamn land. Now I need a lawyer so I can sue the bastards."

"The first thing you need to do is calm down," Cass said. "Yelling and threatening people isn't going to help."

"How the hell am I supposed to calm down when they got my ass locked up in jail for no good reason?"

"They're releasing you with no charges."

Jack looked surprised; then his eyes narrowed with wariness. "When?"

"In a few minutes."

"And no charges?"

"None."

"What about him?" Jack pointed at Dup.

"The same. They are going to hold your gun while the county attorney deals with some ... administrative details, but Hank Cross said you should have it back in a few days."

"Ha!" said Jack. "I knew there'd be a catch. Administrative details, my ass. They take a man's gun away, there's no telling what they'll try next. You mark my words, this thing ain't over. Not by a long shot."

CHAPTER 12

*D*estiny was calling Clancy Meeker. He was sure of it this time. He'd heard its call before, calls that proved to be false echoes leading to disappointment and heartache, but now, finally at the age of forty, he thought this felt like the real thing.

Clancy Meeker was first and foremost a salesman. The product or service had never mattered. Clancy could sell it. He had sold cars and insurance and vacuum cleaners. He had worked the kiosks at the mall in Duluth, peddling cell phones and leather goods and hand-painted ties and socks. As a boy he had gone door to door selling Girl Scout cookies for his sister because she couldn't close a sale and he could. Yes, Clancy could close a sale with the best of them, but despite that talent good fortune had always eluded him, and the common thread running through all the disappointment had been the fact that the failures were never Clancy's fault. There had been bad bosses and unfair competition. There had been shoddy products and customers who took perfectly good products and then refused to pay. Once he had been cleaning up with a miracle cream guaranteed to remove wrinkles and rejuvenate the skin, only to have the government declare it a carcinogen and put him out of business. At times it felt like a great conspiracy by a world jealous of Clancy's talent to deprive him of happiness.

But now Clancy was selling something totally different, something immune to the whims of bosses or poor workmanship, something his customers would soon find irresistible, even if they didn't know it yet. He was selling himself. Clancy Meeker was running for Congress.

To be sure, it was a daunting task, made more so by the fact that he was trying to unseat Clausen Diggs, a ten-term incumbent. Diggs was blessed with a silver tongue, a huge campaign chest, and a willingness to say anything with little regard for the truth so long as it endeared him to voters. That had served him well in the U.S. House of Representatives for twenty years now, but his luck was about to run out. Clausen Diggs was about to get a lesson in salesmanship from Clancy Meeker.

It had been surprisingly easy to gain party endorsement, much easier than he had thought. Apparently, everyone else contemplating a run had weighed the prospects of beating Diggs and decided to await a better opportunity. When Clancy approached the party's district chairman about running, Mike Lands acted as if party endorsement was handed out as casually as campaign buttons.

"Sure, we'll endorse you," Lands said without hesitation. "It's always good to have a warm body on the ballot in case Diggs gets hit by a truck the week before the election. But don't expect any money. You're on your own there. The party funds are all earmarked for the races where we have a chance."

Clancy didn't much appreciate being typecast as either a warm body or a lost cause, but he took it in stride. After all, the powers in the party hadn't yet seen Clancy close a sale, so their thinking would surely come around once his campaign was under way.

Nor did Clancy enjoy much respect from the home front. When he told his wife, Nadeen, of his plans, she burst into laughter. When he asked what was so funny, she managed to say, "You ... Congress ..." before surrendering to laughter again.

Once more Clancy took it in stride. They could underestimate and mock him all they wanted, but they'd change their tune once he'd closed the sale. Toward that end, he then gave serious thought to the main pitch of his campaign, concluding that the winningest strategy was to sell manliness. The voters of woodsy northern

Minnesota would surely want to send a man's man to Washington. Sadly though, the word that best described Clancy was "average." He was average in height and slight in build and closer to homely than handsome. His physical presence would never invoke thoughts of an extra-large jock strap, but he also understood that remedying all that averageness was just a matter of packaging and marketing.

His first move was to trade in his minivan—real men don't drive minivans—for a pickup. Next, his market research revealed that manliness intersected with one issue more than any other: gun rights. This was initially a problem, as Clancy didn't own a gun. He had never hunted and didn't feel a great need for personal protection, but now he clearly had a need, one that was easily met with a trip to a sporting goods store where he made five strategic purchases. The first two items on his shopping list were a twelve-gauge shotgun and a deer rifle. The next was ammunition for both guns. His fourth purchase was a rack for the rear window of his pickup where his new guns would hang for voters everywhere to see. He then paused before making his final purchase, wondering if it might be a bit over the top, before deciding that it was impossible to be over the top in politics.

At the checkout Clancy paid for his purchases, gathered up his guns and ammo and rack, then donned his new coonskin cap. The clerk smirked and asked, "You supposed to be Daniel Boone or Davy Crockett?"

Clancy just smiled. It didn't matter. Either one worked. The important thing was that the clerk got the message the new packaging was meant to convey.

With his image makeover complete, Clancy charged boldly onto the campaign trail, only to be quickly buffeted by headwinds blowing from Clausen Diggs and his lackeys. The man was a master at pandering and half-truths, and Clancy's cash disadvantage also became apparent. Mostly, though, it was a matter of Diggs dominating every venue and hogging all the limelight, denying Clancy a stage on which to strut his stuff.

But now destiny had smiled on Clancy, giving him the stage he needed. It was as if the gods of politics had built it just for him. Over breakfast in a restaurant that morning, he had overheard two fellows talking about an incident the day before out at Forgotten Lake. A property owner had been arrested, his gun taken away. Clancy spent the rest of the morning gathering information, and now he was convinced that he had the perfect issue with which to take on Diggs. Diggs had given only lip service to gun rights, trying to play both sides of the street, and now Clancy was going to clobber him with it. The government was taking guns away from law-abiding citizens. The situation clearly called for a man's man. Clancy had found his starring role and Forgotten Lake would be his stage.

CHAPTER 13

The run of fine weather came to an end. The day began cloudy with a cool breeze out of the northeast and by nine that morning a steady rain was falling on Forgotten Lake. It was a gloom to match Jack Baird's mood as he still brooded over his arrest, despite having been released without charges. By ten Cass'd had enough. She told Jack that she was driving into Forsythe. She had some shopping to do, a few things she needed to pick up.

"I gotta go in tomorrow," Jack said. "I could get whatever you need then." He viewed any trip into Forsythe to be a disagreeable mission, and unnecessary trips were to be avoided at all cost. "What is it you need, anyway?"

"Girl stuff."

"Oh."

Girl stuff proved to be an ample justification for an extra trip, and now as she drove, the wipers thumping a steady beat against the rain, she felt only a touch of guilt over not telling Jack her chief reason for going to town. And she did have some things to pick up, so there was an element of truth in what she had said, but she also had failed to mention that she was meeting Brian Walsh for lunch. It had been Brian's idea, arranged while they were waiting for Jack's release from the sheriff's office. Brian was claiming part ownership of the silly dam business, and he also claimed to be on Jack's side, but beyond that she had no idea what he planned to do about it. She also suspected that Jack's situation wasn't the limit of Brian's interest, but given Jack's foul mood and his current distrust of anyone from the government, she thought it best to discover Brian's intentions before saying anything to her father.

They were to meet at the Jack Pine Broiler, a sports bar featuring a fake log exterior and a knotty pine interior with a wide-screen TV for almost every line of sight. Brian's pickup was already in the parking lot when she pulled in, and once inside she joined him at the table where he was already seated. The midday crowd was light, with fewer than half the tables taken, and a waitress promptly appeared with menus.

To the waitress's query about drinks, Brian raised his eyebrows to Cass and asked, "Something from the bar?"

"Are you?"

"I'll have a beer," he said.

She ordered chardonnay. They then made small talk about the weather until their drinks came, at which time Cass ordered a chef's salad and Brian ordered a burger. After a sip of wine, she asked, "So what's your agenda?"

He winced. "Agenda sounds so formal, like a business meeting."

"And you had something else in mind? A tryst perhaps?"

"Um, well ... no. I just thought we should talk. About Jack's problem."

Cass was quietly amused at his apparent discomfort with her frankness. "Okay, let's talk."

He paused for a gulp of beer before going on. "I ... uh ... I can't see Jack letting go of this thing, so I think his best course of action is to apply for a dam permit."

"But you said yourself that the odds are against him getting one."

"Typically, yeah," he nodded, "but in this case I think sound environmental arguments can be made for a dam, and while it's a complicated process, I'd be willing to help."

She eyed him for a moment. "Why would you do that?"

"It's my job. A big part of what I do, the most satisfying part actually, is helping property owners deal with land use and environmental regs. Those things can be awfully intimidating if you don't know your way around them."

"But what about dear Commissioner Dugan? He seems pretty intent on getting rid of the dam. You may have sound arguments, but politics has a way of skewing good policy."

He shrugged. "Yeah, there's that, but I'd like to try anyway. I'm a civil engineer, so I can make a pretty strong case for a dam. And besides, if Jack doesn't go the permit route, he's likely to end up in some serious trouble with the law."

With that their food came and they lapsed into silence as they started eating. After a minute, she poked a fork into her salad but instead of taking a bite she looked up. "What about you? Aren't you taking some risk too? Seems like a county employee going up against a commissioner isn't exactly a career-enhancing move."

He chewed for a moment before answering. "Sometimes you have to take risks, especially when avoiding risk means abandoning something you believe to be right."

"Ah! A *principled* civil engineer, no less."

His grin was sheepish. "Sorry, didn't mean to sound so ... righteous."

"No, that's okay. The world could stand some honest righteousness these days." She paused for a sip of wine. "So why are you telling me all this? What do you want me to do?"

"Talk to Jack. I know I'm not his favorite person right now, and I'm hoping you can convince him that I'm on his side and that he should work with me."

She nodded. "I can do that."

"Thanks." He paused, then cleared his throat. "I was also hoping that maybe we could get together some evening, you and I, to, um ..."

Cass smiled. "Why, Mr. Walsh, you did have a tryst in mind, after all."

He blushed. "If you'd rather not—"

"No, no, I'd like that. Especially if it helps put an end to this stupid dam business."

"And we will," Brian said. "I'm an optimist. I think things are gonna turn for the better."

* * *

"I think things are gonna turn for the worse," said Jack Baird. "Don't see any way around it."

Dup Dingle shook his head. "Goddamn govmint."

Dup had shown up at Jack's door soon after Cass left for town. He'd come across the lake through the rain in his open boat, his inadequate rain gear consisting of an old ball cap and a plastic garbage bag with holes poked for his arms and head, so he arrived soaked and shivering. Jack draped an old towel over one of the wooden chairs around the big oak table for Dup to sit on; then he administered his preferred remedy for a chill: beer. Now they were both seated at the table, each working on a second beer, and while Dup had stopped shivering he still looked to Jack like a drowned rat. His spirits were low too. Despite his mean existence, Dup had never tangled with the law, and his arrest and brief incarceration had left him badly shaken. He understood that there was great risk in exotic and rowdy places like Duluth, but to be snatched up by the authorities at Forgotten Lake—his home, his refuge—left him feeling violated and vulnerable. He had come across the lake in the rain with the hope that the only man he could think to turn to for reassurance would tell him that things were going to be alright. But instead Jack had said he expected things to get worse.

"You ain't thinking about putting your dam in again, are you?" Dup asked.

"Not sure what I'm gonna do just yet. Gotta figure some things out before I do anything."

"But Jack, you put it back and they're gonna throw your ass in jail, sure as hell. That judge said so."

"I didn't say I was gonna put it back," Jack said. "I said I'm gonna think things through, but I'll tell you one thing for sure, I ain't gonna lie down and let 'em walk all over me. You do that, there's no stopping 'em next time. A man's gotta take a stand somewhere."

Dup looked unhappy at the prospect of taking a stand. "I just wish things'd get back to normal around here. Hell, it's getting so I can hardly sleep at night for fear they're gonna come and haul me away."

"Well, why don't you lock your door for a change?"

Dup shook his head. "Won't help. They'll just bust her down, and then I'll have to get me a new door on top a everything else."

"You're getting to be a real paranoid, you know that?" Jack said.

Dup's eyebrows knitted in confusion. "A pair a what?"

Before Jack could answer, the sound of a car door slamming could be heard from outside. "You expecting someone?" Dup asked.

"It's probably Cass. She went into Forsythe to do some shopping."

But a moment later it was Hamilton Madison who came around the lakeside of the house and stepped onto the deck. He was dressed in his usual camo attire but on this day he had added a vinyl poncho—also in camo—to guard against the rain. Once inside, he shrugged out of the wet poncho to reveal a holstered semiautomatic pistol strapped around his waist.

"You plan on shooting somebody?" Jack asked, pointing at the gun.

"Maybe," Ham said with an enigmatic smile. "Way things been going around here lately, a man's gotta be prepared for about anything."

"Well, you ain't gonna shoot anybody here," Jack said, "so sit down and have a beer."

Ham agreed that for the moment a beer was preferred over gunfire. Jack fetched three more beers from the nearby refrigerator and they settled down around the table. After a long pull on his beer, Ham looked at Jack and asked, "Those assholes give your gun back yet?"

Jack shook his head.

"Well, I wouldn't hold my breath if I were you. Somewhere along the line these cops got it in their heads that they should be the only ones with guns. That might work for some pussy Europeans, but it ain't gonna work in America. No way, Jose.'"

Jack shrugged. "I don't like them pushing me around, but what the hell can a fella do? They got the law and the courts and everything on their side. Ain't exactly a fair fight."

"That's just what I come by to tell you," Ham said. "The fight's about to get a damn sight fairer. Help's on the way. I've been in touch with some folks who hold the Second Amendment dear."

"What? You been talking to the NRA?" asked Dup.

"No." Ham waved a dismissive hand. "The NRA talks a good game, but at the end of the day talking's all they do. They're really nothing more than a bunch of lobbyists. No, you wanna get something done, you need men of action, true patriots." He paused before continuing in a hushed tone. "What you need, Jack, is militiamen, and I happen to know a bunch of 'em."

"Militiamen are coming here?" Jack asked.

Ham nodded. "True patriots to the rescue."

"Where they coming from?"

"All over," Ham said. "Texas and Idaho to name a couple places."

Jack studied his beer for a moment. "I'm not sure I want those fellas on my property any more than I want cops around."

"Fine," said Ham. "You wanna let the government walk all over you and take away your constitutional rights, then go ahead and turn down help from the only real friends you got. But if you're ready to take a stand, then these boys'll stand with you to the end."

An uneasy silence hung in the air for a long moment before Dup Dingle said, "I just wish things'd get back to normal around here."

* * *

After lunch with Brian, Cass took care of her shopping and now she climbed into her car for the return trip to Forgotten Lake. She slipped the key into the ignition, but instead of starting the engine she sat back, musing over something that had nagged her since lunch. She had agreed to meet Brian again the next night. He suggested a different restaurant in town and said that he would pick her up at Forgotten Lake at six. It sounded a lot like a date, but they had both avoided the word, framing it instead as a meeting, ostensibly to again discuss Jack's situation. Deal with the business at hand, nothing more. Still, it felt like a date to Cass, and she was fine with that, and she suspected that a date was what Brian had in mind too, but for some reason he was unable to say so. Probably shyness, she thought. He did seem painfully shy, though in her view shyness in a man wasn't a bad thing, and there were other things about him she found appealing as well. He wasn't drop-dead handsome, which was fine, as she thought most men who were to be a pain, but he was attractive in a comfortable, unassuming way. And despite his shyness, he seemed so sincere, and sincerity was another quality Cass liked in a man. So she had agreed to meet him the next night, and while they weren't calling it a date, she found herself hoping it would turn into one. She did, however, say that she would meet him in town, that until Jack's reaction to Brian's offer of help was known, it was perhaps best that Brian avoid Forgotten Lake.

She turned the key, starting the engine, but as she reached for the gearshift lever she was startled by the ringtone of her cell phone. There was no cell service at Forgotten Lake, so the phone hadn't been interrupting her there as it did in New Orleans. In just a few days she'd grown accustomed to being free of that, and now it seemed a harsh intrusion. She picked it up and looked at the screen and sighed. She was tempted to let the call go, but then she answered.

"Hello, Mother."

"So he got arrested," Diane Baird said. "It was only a matter of time, I suppose. The shock is that it didn't happen long ago."

"Just so you know, he was released without charges," Cass said. "And how'd you find out, anyway? I wasn't aware that it'd made the news down in the Cities."

"It didn't. I have people up there I stay in touch with, people who keep me up on what's happening."

"I didn't think you cared about what happens at Forgotten Lake."

"I don't, but I care about you, Cassandra. With all that craziness going on, someone's likely to get shot or something, and I don't want it to be you. Actually, that's the reason I called. I think you should come down and stay with me in the Cities until it's time for you to go back to New Orleans. There's so much more to do here. We could go shopping, and Gerald could take us out to dinner and the theater, and you'd be so much safer."

Cass shuddered at the thought of spending more time with her mother and Gentleman Gerald. "I feel perfectly safe at the lake, Mother."

"Dear God, you've got your father's stubbornness. Well, at the very least, we can get together in Duluth. Gerald has some business up there the day after tomorrow. I think I'll ride along and we can meet for lunch."

"If you're coming that far, why not come all the way to Forgotten Lake. I'll fix a nice lunch." Cass knew how preposterous her suggestion was, but she made it to needle her mother.

"You'll never catch me alive at that god-awful lake again. Duluth is as close as I'm going to get. Meet me at that Mexican place in Canal Park at 12:30 and don't be late."

With that Diane Baird broke the connection, leaving her daughter to stare in wonder at her phone. Cass had just been summarily ordered to Duluth for lunch, and she felt only a little guilty over her next thought: Forgotten Lake was a better place without her mother.

CHAPTER 14

The rain had finally stopped and a few breaks were showing in the morning clouds, but it was still cool and wet on the deck so Cass and Jack had eaten their breakfast inside. They sat back now with their coffee and Cass steeled herself before raising a subject that her father was sure to resist.

"Have you given any thought to applying for a permit for your dam?" she asked.

Jack responded with a quizzical look. "No point in trying. They'll never give me one."

"I'm not so sure. I've, um, been looking into it a bit, and I think there's a fair chance you might get one."

His eyes narrowed. "You've been looking into it, huh? Just exactly where you been looking?"

Cass paused, then pressed on. "Actually, I had lunch with Brian Walsh in Forsythe yesterday and—"

"Walsh! That son of a bitch's been against my dam from day one. He's the one who told me I'd have to be as big as the Tennessee Valley Authority to get a permit. Talking to him is like sneaking around behind my back and meeting with the enemy."

Cass was becoming annoyed now. "He's not the enemy, Dad. He wants to help, and he happens to be an engineer, so he can deal with all the technical stuff in the permitting process."

"I ain't buying it." Jack shook his head. "Walsh works for the government, and right now I don't trust anybody that's got anything to do with the goddamn government."

"At least talk to him and hear what he has to say. Talking can't hurt, and as it happens I'm meeting him again tonight so—"

"Another meeting with the enemy, huh? Next thing you'll probably be dragging your mother into it too."

Cass laughed. "Well, actually, I'm meeting Mother for lunch in Duluth tomorrow."

"Aw, Jesus H. Christ!"

"It has nothing to do with you, Dad. She's going to be in Duluth with her, um ... friend, and she wants to get together, that's all."

Jack snorted. "Her friend, huh? By that I assume you mean that fella she's shacked up with."

"That's not something we're going to discuss. Let's stick to the topic at hand, which is a permit for your dam. If you're serious about the dam, then you should apply for a permit and accept Brian's offer of help."

Jack paused, studying his coffee mug. "To be honest with you, I'm kinda losing my enthusiasm for the dam. All the fun's gone out of it. But I still hate the government pushing me around—that's the thing that's hard to get past."

"Well, if that's how you feel, then forget the dam and the government'll leave you alone."

"But then they will've won."

Cass sighed. Her mother was right about one thing: Jack Baird was a truly stubborn man. She decided to let the matter of the dam ride for a while, hoping that with time her father might get past his anger. She got up and cleared the breakfast dishes to the kitchen and was preparing to wash them when she heard a car door slam. She walked to the back door and peered out the window at a man in a coonskin cap standing next to a pickup.

"Who is it?" Jack asked.

"Don't know. Were you perhaps expecting Davy Crockett?"

"Huh?"

"Whoever it is, he's coming around the front."

Moments later the man came onto the deck and Jack stepped out to meet him. Cass followed. The man was looking out at the lake, but at the sound of the door opening, he turned to face them. "Beautiful place you have here, absolutely beautiful."

Jack eyed him warily. "Thanks. What's your business?"

The man held out his hand. "Clancy Meeker, candidate for the United States House of Representatives. And I assume you're Jack Baird, famed freedom fighter."

Jack hesitated, then shook the man's hand. "You a Democrat or Republican?"

"Does it matter?"

Jack shrugged. "I reckon one's as bad as the other."

"Well then, you and I are in total agreement, Mr. Baird, because the issues you've raised transcend petty party politics. You've done a great service to the nation and the Constitution, sir. We are all in your debt."

Jack squinted. "What the hell are you talking about?"

"Your courageous stand against tyranny. Your refusal to be trampled by a government bent on plundering our Second Amendment rights."

Cass snickered. Jack gave her a quick scowl, then asked Meeker, "Are you one of them militia fellas Hamilton Madison was talking about?"

"Who's Hamilton Madison?"

Jack cocked his head to one side. "Just exactly what is it you want?"

"I'm here, sir, because our destinies are joined. We are fellow travelers on the same road. We are warriors bound together in the battle for freedom."

"Look here, buster," said Jack, "you got ten seconds to drop all this gibberish and give me a good reason why I shouldn't run you off my property."

"Getting right to the point! I like that. I knew you wouldn't stand for pussyfooting around and—"

"Five seconds."

"Right. I'm here, Mr. Baird, because I'm running for Congress and the government's been pushing you around and I think we can help each other out."

"And how we gonna do that?" Jack looked skeptical.

"By shining the light of truth on Forgotten Lake. By exposing the government's tyranny for all to see."

"You're talking gibberish again."

"Sorry. What I'd like to do is stage a campaign rally here at Forgotten Lake, at the site of your dam, complete with full media coverage."

Jack winced. "Now why the hell would I want all those people running around on my property? Seems like you'd get all the benefit and I'd get all the headaches."

"I don't agree, sir," Meeker said. "It's true that I stand to benefit, but I believe the benefits will be mutual, because you'll get to poke your finger in the government's eye and have it shown on television."

Cass had been looking on, barely able to keep from laughing at the farce playing out before her, but now she saw a change in her father's expression. His impatience with Meeker had been growing, but now he seemed to be mulling over the man's proposition. She imagined him weighing his privacy at Forgotten Lake, something he held dear, against the chance to poke his finger in the government's eye. Privacy was important, but fighting the government was in her father's DNA. She had been hopeful that Jack's waning enthusiasm for his dam would cause him to back down, but now this clueless politician in a coonskin cap was stoking the fire again. She no longer felt like laughing.

"Let me give it some thought," Jack said.

"I'll need to know fairly soon," Meeker said.

"I'll let you know by tomorrow."

Oh dear, thought Cass.

CHAPTER 15

"*A*re you nuts?" asked Zack Buchwald.

Brian Walsh wasn't surprised by his office manager's reaction. "No, I'm not nuts. I'm just doing my job."

"Coulda fooled me. Looks more like you're trying to *lose* your job."

"Look, Zack, the law provides for a permitting process, so if Jack Baird wants to apply for one, then he has every right to do so. To summarily deny him the opportunity to even apply could be construed as enforcing the law capriciously and leave us open to a lawsuit."

Zack sank into the chair across the desk from Brian and shook his head. "I still say you're nuts. Have I mentioned that Commissioner 'No Sweat' Dugan calls me at least twice a day? You can be pretty damn sure he's not calling to pass the time of day or to inquire about my health."

Brian shrugged. "A dam on Forgotten Lake has environmental merit, I've said so all along, and it deserves to be proved or disproved on technical grounds. If we allow the process to become politicized, then we should all lose our jobs."

"Thanks all the same, but I'd just as soon hang onto mine." Zack pondered a moment. "Has Baird told you in so many words that he wants a permit?"

Brian hesitated. "Um ... actually, I've been dealing mostly with his daughter."

"What?"

"She has Baird's power of attorney. And she's very capable. She's an economist."

"I don't care if she's a brain surgeon," Zack said. "What you're telling me is that the actual property owner hasn't requested a permit."

"I'm meeting with his daughter again tonight. I'm hopeful that she'll convey a formal request at that time."

"You're hopeful, huh?" Zack pointed a finger at Brian. "If you're smart, you'll be hoping Baird decides to get outta the dam business altogether."

* * *

Cass met Brian at the Forsythe Country Club where the restaurant, with a complete lack of imagination, was named the Nineteenth Hole. It was nicer than the name implied though, with wide second-story windows overlooking the eighteenth green and tree-lined fairways extending into the distance. As they made their way to their table, she felt his hand on the small of her back. It was a gentle touch, but it also felt vaguely intimate, and she wondered if he might finally get past his shyness with her. They ordered drinks—scotch on the rocks for her, a martini for him—then they studied the menu until their drinks came. The waitress took their food order—shrimp and linguini with Alfredo sauce for Cass, a steak for Brian—and after she had gone, Cass asked, "So do you play golf?"

"Not well. You?"

"Not at all. I grew up on a lake. I'm a water girl."

"Yeah, I'm the same way. Guess that's why I live on a lake now."

"You live on a lake?" she said, surprised. "I don't know why, but I just assumed that you lived here in town."

"I did my first year back, in an apartment, but first chance I had I bought a lake cabin."

"Which lake?"

He grinned. "Round Lake. A very distinctive name shared by a couple hundred other Minnesota lakes, but my particular Round Lake is just five miles from here, so it's very handy for me. And the cabin's small, just two bedrooms, nothing like your place on Forgotten Lake."

"Forgotten Lake was once called Long Lake, which Minnesota has quite a few of too," she said. "It was my grandfather who renamed it."

"I think I knew that." He paused to sip his martini. "Did you, ah, get a chance to talk to Jack about applying for a permit?"

"Yeah." Her expression soured.

"And?"

"Pretty much as I expected. He didn't wildly embrace the idea, but then he surprised me by saying that his enthusiasm for the dam was waning, that he might forget about it altogether, which to my way of thinking would be the best possible outcome."

"I absolutely agree," he said. "That'd solve a lot of problems. So do you think it'll happen?"

She sighed. "I was hoping so, but then along came Clancy Meeker."

"Who?"

Cass related the would-be politician's visit to Forgotten Lake that morning and his desire to hold a campaign rally at the site of Jack's dam. "Just when it seemed like Dad was ready to back down, this guy comes along and gets him all stoked up again."

"Is the rally gonna happen?"

She nodded. "This morning Dad told Meeker that he'd let him know by tomorrow, but then he called him just before I left to come here and gave him the green light. Now he's all fired up about putting the dam in again and poking his finger in the government's eye."

"That's not gonna help." He frowned. "I don't recall hearing of this Meeker guy. Is he a serious candidate?"

"Serious? He goes around in a coonskin cap, for God's sake. No, he's not serious, but he could be dangerous. I'm afraid Dad thinks he can use Meeker to counter Dugan and get away with doing whatever he likes."

"Not good. If he puts the dam in again without a permit, he'll likely end up back in jail, and I don't think he'll get out quite so easily next time."

"A dandy prospect, indeed."

With that their food came and they lapsed into silence as they began eating. After a bit Cass glanced up. Brian wore a frown as he ate and she wondered if the frown was a sign of concern for her father or if he was worrying about something else. She continued to get vibes from him, vibes that seemed to hint at an interest in a deeper relationship, but then the vibes would be interrupted with lapses of hemming and hawing. Perhaps it was time, she thought, to send some clear vibes of her own.

"I'd like to see your cabin sometime," she said.

He nodded as he finished chewing. "Yeah, we'll do that."

"Why not tonight?"

He seemed surprised; then he smiled. "Yeah, tonight, for sure."

* * *

She followed his pickup in her car. They turned off the highway a few miles north of Forsythe and followed a gravel road for another mile or so before coming to his cabin. The sun was just setting, reflecting orange across the still water of the small lake. The cabin was set in birch and pine, trees that offered a buffer between neighboring cabins that were no closer than fifty yards on either side. In front of the cabin a short dock extended out from the stony shore, an open aluminum boat with an outboard motor moored to it. As Cass took it all in, she couldn't help a smile. Brian Walsh's retreat was a scaled-down version of her father's on Forgotten Lake.

Once everyone's intentions were known, once the vibrations were made clear, things moved along nicely. A quick tour of the property was followed by an equally quick tour of the cabin, complete with the requisite comment on the appropriateness of knotty pine for lake cabin interiors. Next came drinks and small talk, a refilling of drinks, a first kiss, then a second and a third, some fumbling with buttons, then at last to bed.

Now he rolled off her with a sigh and lay on his back, breathing softly and staring up at the ceiling. He had been gentle enough, she thought, but there had been no hemming and hawing to his lovemaking, and she slid close, savoring the warmth of his skin next to her own. After a time he chuckled.

"What?" she asked.

"It occurs to me that I'm not even sure of your name. Is Cass short for Cassidy?"

"Nothing so trendy. It's Cassandra."

"Ah, Cassandra. Mysterious and exotic."

She laughed. "That's me, Cassandra, the mysterious and exotic economist. And being mysterious and exotic, I should probably be starting for home."

"Why?"

Why, indeed, she wondered. She could imagine her father's reaction should she return to Forgotten Lake in the morning. He hadn't liked her talking to the enemy, so sleeping with him would surely be worse. But on the other hand, she wasn't looking forward to driving back in the dark, and she was, after all, a forty-year-old woman, accustomed to living independently, who didn't really care what her father thought. Without a word she turned to face him and his arm encircled her, drawing her close.

CHAPTER 16

They came in the night. They came while Cass and Brian slept in each other's arms, while Jack Baird slept alone in his log home, while Dup Dingle slept fretfully, fearful that the authorities would break down the door of his humble cabin at any moment. They came to the south end of Forgotten Lake where there was only a footpath along the Bumble River through a hundred yards of woods to the lakeshore and the on-and-off site of Jack's dam. There was no road to the shore but since their vehicles were all four-wheel drive—two Jeep Cherokees and three pickups—they simply drove along the shallow river's stony bed to the lake, and there they set up their command post. They worked quietly and efficiently in the dark. Campers were mounted on two of the pickups and four tents were erected for those the campers wouldn't accommodate. Coolers with iced-down food and beer were unloaded. A camp stove was set up, and soon the aromas of frying bacon and brewing coffee mixed in the pine-scented air. A campfire was built and they gathered around it, eating bacon sandwiches and drinking coffee laced with whiskey. They had driven many miles and they were tired, but now they had arrived and they were ready. Sentries were set and the others retired to tents and campers to sleep and await the dawn.

* * *

As usual, Dup Dingle was up by six that morning. After a breakfast of instant coffee and a Little Debbie, he collected his bait—leeches swimming in a jar of water—from his refrigerator, gathered up his rod and reel, and made his way down to the lake and his boat. A dock was a luxury Dup couldn't afford, so he simply pulled the boat onto a sandy patch on the shore and tied it off to a nearby birch. Now he loaded his gear, untied the boat, and shoved off. His outboard motor sputtered to life on the third pull and he set out across the lake's glassy surface. A thick fog had settled over the lake and the shoreline quickly disappeared into the gray opacity. He continued across the lake until the island loomed out of the fog, and there he turned south and followed the island's shore to its southern tip and then a bit farther on before shutting the motor down and throwing out the anchor. Land had once more disappeared into the fog on all sides, but Dup knew the lake well and he knew exactly where he was. It was a favorite fishing spot, a submerged rock pile, two hundred yards south of the island with the Bumble River outlet another quarter mile to the south. He reached into the jar and grabbed a leech, allowing it to sucker onto his finger before deftly hooking it; then he attached a bobber and cast his line out.

He fished patiently in his quiet fog-bound world for nearly half an hour before the bobber went down. He played out line, giving the fish time to swallow the leech; then he slowly reeled in, feeling for the fish, and when he felt a tug he snapped the rod back, setting the hook. He hoped for a big walleye, because that's what he always hoped for, but it felt small as he reeled it to the boat. What he actually landed wasn't a walleye at all but a nice-sized perch. Dup nodded his satisfaction. Walleye may have been the hope, but perch tasted just as good. He stringered the fish and tied it off to the side of the boat; then he rebaited and cast his line again.

The sun was higher in the sky now and burning down through the fog. Soon the rocks and trees of the island's southern tip reappeared and a few minutes later the south shore of the lake slowly emerged too. Vague shapes loomed gradually into trees and ... Dup's eyes widened. He blinked, unsure of what he was seeing, and then he was sure.

"Holy shit!" he said. He quickly reeled in his line, pulled the stringer into the boat, weighed anchor, and yanked the starter cord on the motor.

* * *

Jack Baird took his morning coffee on the deck. The sun had burned off much of the fog and promised a fine day, though his mood was no match for that promise. The first thing he had noted upon rising was that Cass's car was gone, that she hadn't returned from her meeting with Brian Walsh. Some meeting, he thought. Oh, he knew that Cass was a grown woman and could do as she pleased, but did she have to go around consorting with the enemy? Of course, Cass claimed Walsh wasn't the enemy, that he really wanted to help, but Jack remained skeptical about that. Walsh may think he wants to help, but in Jack's experience help from the government was usually more trouble than it was worth.

A slamming car door sounded from the back and moments later Cass rounded the corner of the house and stepped onto the deck. "And where might you be sneaking in from?" Jack asked.

"I'm not *sneaking* from anywhere."

"I see. And I suppose it's none of my business where you were all night."

She stared at him for a moment. "Yeah, you have a right to know, and as a matter of fact I spent the night at Brian's cabin."

Jack snorted. "He still claiming he wants to help?"

"He can't help if you won't let him, Dad, if you won't apply for a permit."

"Hell, they'll never give me a permit, not as long as Dugan's on the warpath."

She shrugged. "Your choice. I'm going to shower and change and head for Duluth."

"Duluth?"

"Yes, Duluth. Did you forget that I'm meeting Mother for lunch?"

Jack's expression soured, but their attention was then drawn to the sound of an approaching motorboat. They looked to the lake as Dup Dingle's boat came in, slowed, and bumped against the dock. Dup quickly hopped out, tied the boat off, then raced up to the house, and when he got to the deck he was winded.

"What the hell's got you so worked up this early in the day?" Jack asked.

Dup took a moment to catch his breath, but then he glanced at Cass and broke into a wide grin that revealed his missing teeth. "Morning, Miss Cass."

"Good morning, Dup. How are you?"

"I'm fine, Miss Cass, just fine." He beamed for a moment longer; then he seemed to remember why he was there and he turned to Jack. "There's a buncha guys down at the south enda the lake where the Bumble lets out."

"What the hell you talking about?" Jack said.

"That can't be Meeker's rally already, can it?" Cass asked.

"Nah," Jack shook his head. "That's not for another day or so." He looked to Dup. "Just go slow and tell me exactly what you saw."

Dup took a breath. "Well, I was fishing, see, and it was foggy so you couldn't see shit, and then the fog she burned off and there they all were. Jack, there's tents and trucks and guys walking around and—"

"How many?"

Dup shrugged. "Didn't stop to count 'em, but I'd guess there's at least six, maybe more. You s'pose it's them militia fellas Ham Madison was talking about?"

Jack nodded. "Could be."

"Militia?" said Cass. "What's this about militia?"

As if on cue, the sound of another car door slamming came from the back and moments later Hamilton Madison stepped onto the deck sporting a wide grin with a holstered pistol once more strapped around his waist. "Morning, folks. Good day for a revolution, huh?"

"We'll just see about that," Jack said. "I take it you know something about a bunch of guys camped down at the south end of the lake."

"I sure do," Ham said. "That's what I came by to tell you. SAM has arrived."

"Sam? Who the hell's Sam? And Dup here said there's more'n one, that there's at least six."

Ham nodded. "Ten, actually, and SAM ain't a guy. SAM stands for Sons of the Alamo Militia."

"Dear God," said Cass.

"And they ain't all guys either," Ham added. "They got a couple women with 'em too, but every last one of 'em can handle a gun. I'll guarantee you that."

"Sons of the Alamo?" Jack said. "They from Texas?"

"Yep. And they're just the start. There's more on the way. I expect a bunch from Idaho to get here this afternoon."

"This is not good, Dad," Cass said. "This can only lead to trouble."

"You're wrong there, missy," said Ham. "The trouble's already here, and it's the government trampling all over our constitutional rights. These folks are our friends. They're here to help. Think of 'em like the cavalry coming to the rescue."

Cass turned to her father. "If this gets out of hand and someone gets hurt, which seems likely given a bunch of people with guns, then you could be held liable because you allowed them on your land."

"Don't listen to her, Jack," Ham said. "That's the kinda thinking that's gonna turn us all into slaves. Goddamn it, it's time to stand up and fight for our freedom."

Cass started to speak again but Jack held up his hand, cutting her off. "You go on and get ready for your trip to Duluth. Go have a nice lunch with your mother, and I'll go down and check these militia fellas out. If I decide they're more trouble than they're worth, then I'll run 'em off, but it's still my land and I'm gonna decide what goes and what doesn't."

"But, Dad—"

"Go on now."

Cass glared at her father, then at Hamilton Madison; then with a shake of her head she turned and walked into the house. After she had gone, Jack said, "Dup, you'd better get on home." He then turned to Ham. "Okay, let's you and me go check out these Sons of the Alamo Militia."

CHAPTER 17

$\mathcal{J}$ack rode with Hamilton Madison to the south end of the lake and along the way he quizzed Ham about the militia. "So you knew they were coming last night?" Jack asked.

"Yep," Ham nodded. "We've been communicating over email for a few days now. I even offered to meet 'em last night and guide 'em to the site, but Major Mike said that wasn't necessary."

"Major Mike?"

"He's the leader of SAM."

"He got a last name?"

Ham shrugged. "I expect he does, but I've never heard it. He just goes by Major Mike."

"You known him long?"

"We've been, shall we say, corresponding for a couple years now, but until I went over there first thing this morning we'd never actually met. I'd heard lots of good stuff about him, but I gotta tell you, Jack, once you meet him face-to-face, you're gonna be impressed. He's one capable dude. You got the A-team on your side now."

"We'll see about that," Jack said.

Ham chuckled. "And speaking of impressive, wait'll you get a look at Wanda."

"Who's Wanda?"

"Major Mike's woman."

"They married?"

"Maybe, maybe not, but there's no doubt that she's his woman." With that they came to the Bumble River and Ham pulled to the side of the road and stopped.

"Dup said they drove their vehicles right up to the shore," Jack said. "What'd they do, drive along the riverbed?"

"Yeah," Ham said. "You wanna do that now?"

"Nah, let's walk."

They climbed from the pickup and started along the path through the woods, but after a short distance Ham stopped. "Wait a sec," he said. "I forgot my action plan in the truck."

"What the hell's your action plan?"

"It's what I've been working on with Major Mike. Hell, Jack, you can't just stumble into an operation like this without a plan. Planning's the difference between a well-run militia and a goddamn mob."

Ham started back to the truck but Jack saw no reason to wait for him. He was on his own land, after all. He walked another thirty yards, then stopped abruptly when a man dressed in camo stepped from behind a tree and aimed a rifle at his head. "You got business here, old-timer?" the man asked.

"Bet your ass, I do, sonny," Jack said. "You Major Mike?"

"Who's asking?"

At that, Hamilton Madison came up from behind. "It's okay, Mack. This is Jack Baird, the property owner."

The man known as Mack considered this for a moment, then slowly lowered the gun. "Sorry about that, old-timer. Can't be too careful, you know."

"Don't call me old-timer," Jack snarled; then he turned to Ham. "What the hell's going on here?"

Ham shrugged. "You just ran into the militia's picket is all. Mack here's just doing his job. Like I've been telling you, these fellas do things the right way."

Jack snorted. "You may think they're doing things right, but I'm getting pretty goddamn tired of having guns pointed at me on my own fucking land."

"Now, Jack, just cool it. Everything's gonna work out real good. You'll see."

Jack and Ham continued along the path and when they got to the shore, they came upon a beehive of activity. Vehicles and tents were arranged in a rough circle along the east bank of the Bumble and at the center of the circle, a field kitchen had been set up. The aroma of fresh-brewed coffee filled the air and a woman worked at a folding table, chopping food in preparation for some sort of meal. At the river five men were busy re-installing the dam. Some were swinging sledge hammers to drive fence posts, others were wielding shovels or hammers, but whatever the tool, each man seemed to have a rifle resting nearby. Several also had pistols strapped around the waist. Everyone, even the woman in the field kitchen, was dressed in camo.

"Which one's Major Mike?" Jack asked.

"Don't see him just now," Ham said.

Jack nodded toward the woman in the field kitchen. "That Wanda?"

"Nope, that's Delores."

One of the men working on the dam came over. "Hey there, Ham." He nodded to Jack. "This the property owner?"

"Yep," Ham said. "Zeke, this is Jack Baird." He looked to Jack. "Zeke here's the number two man in SAM."

Zeke was stocky and sported a buzz cut. He held his hand out to Jack. "Nice to meet you, Jack. Always glad to help a true patriot whenever the government gets too pushy."

"Where's Major Mike?" Ham asked.

Zeke pointed to one of the campers. "He and Wanda are taking a little break." He flashed a knowing grin. "We don't bother them when they're, um ... on break, but he should be out pretty soon." He nodded toward the field kitchen. "You oughta stick around for lunch. Delores is whipping up one of her famous stews."

"We just might do that," Ham said.

With that the door at the back of the camper opened and a man stepped out, looked around, and when his gaze settled on Ham and

Jack and Zeke, he strode toward them. He was a big man, at least six foot three, with broad shoulders and a lean, muscular frame. His square jaw, his wraparound shades, the handgun holstered at his waist—all added to the sense that this was a man who could take care of himself, a man not to be messed with.

"Here's Major Mike," Zeke announced. He then made introductions.

Major Mike silently assessed Jack from behind his shades for a long moment; then he said, "Nice spot you got here, Jack. Scenic and all. Too bad the government's hassling you. A man has a good patch of land like this, he oughta be left alone."

"You'll get no argument from me on that," Jack said.

"Good ground for defending too," Major Mike said. "What with the lake at our back and the woods all around, we could hold off a pretty sizable force."

Jack thought about that for a moment; then he nodded toward the working men. "I see you're putting my dam back in."

"That's just a temporary," Major Mike said. "Once we get the flow stopped, we're gonna build a permanent one outta concrete a few feet downstream."

"Concrete, huh?" Jack seemed impressed.

"Yeah," said Major Mike. "That way if the government comes around and tries to take it out, they won't have an easy time of it." He paused for a grin. "Of course they'll have to mess with us too, and that'll slow 'em down even more."

Jack smiled as he contemplated the look on the faces of the county boys and that asshole deputy when the saw a new concrete dam defended by the men of SAM.

The door of the camper swung open and the eyes of every man in the camp turned to look as a woman stepped out, then walked toward Major Mike and the others. In her own way Wanda was as impressive as Major Mike. She was nearly as tall, close to six feet, and while her body contours were markedly different, she seemed every bit as fit. Her bleached hair was pulled back in an unruly ponytail, and where Major Mike's wraparound shades added to a sense of

strength, Wanda's seemed to evoke mystery. She was dressed like
the others, but Wanda's camo also conveyed an ironic contradic-
tion. The point behind camouflage, after all, is blending in, conceal-
ment, but Wanda's clothing seemed bent on revelation and drawing
attention. Her pants clung snugly to her long legs and the swell of
her butt and her narrow waist. Her top was equally true to a camouflage scheme with its drab dapples of brown and green, but here
the irony only grew stronger. The top fitted as snugly as the pants
and featured a scooped neckline that revealed much of her ample
breasts. She had actually dabbed a few blotches of camo face paint
to the bared portions, but once more that only served to draw attention as she walked up to Major Mike and slipped a possessive arm
around his waist.

Introductions were made, with Jack struggling to keep his
gaze at eye level and not drift down to Wanda's bosom. Hamilton
Madison then raised the spiral notebook he'd been carrying and said,
"Maybe we oughta spend some time on the plan."

Major Mike nodded. "We're close to ready here. The main thing
is to get the new concrete dam done as quickly as possible."

"But what about Jack's gun?" Ham said. "That's what this is all
about, the goddamn government confiscating a law-abiding citizen's
gun, and on his own property to boot. Sure, the dam's important,
but there's no Second Amendment guarantee that a man can build
a dam. This is about the freedom to bear arms."

"You're right, of course," said Major Mike, "but if it comes to
a confrontation, and it most likely will, then it's important that it
happen on ground of our choosing. We try to get Jack's gun back
first thing, we gotta go to them and they'll have the advantage. But
if we draw the line here with the dam, then they gotta come to us,
to ground we can defend. The advantage will be ours."

Ham pondered this for a moment, then nodded his agreement
and turned to Jack. "What'd I tell you, Jack? These fellas know what
the hell they're doing."

Now it was Major Mike who turned to Jack. "You okay with
this, Jack? It's your land, so you've got the final say. You're the boss."

Jack hesitated only a moment. "Aw, what the hell. I'm not up for shooting anybody, but I'm tired of getting pushed around. Let's do it."

"Good," said Major Mike. "And don't worry about any shooting. We're very disciplined. If there's any shooting, they'll be the ones to start it." He pointed to logs that had been arranged as seating around a campfire. "Let's sit down over there and go over the particulars."

They discussed particulars for nearly an hour; then they dined on Delores's stew. Later, as they drove away, Ham turned to Jack. "Pretty impressive, huh?"

Jack thought a moment. "We talking about the militia or Wanda's tits?"

* * *

"Militia?" Diane Baird's eyes were wide with horror. "From Texas?"

Cass immediately regretted mentioning the militia's arrival at Forgotten Lake. She had meant to say nothing, but her mother had angered her with badgering questions about happenings at the lake and in a fit of pique, she had blurted it out. And now she resented her own anger. She didn't want to be angry. She wanted to get back to the happy frame of mind she had awakened with that morning in Brian Walsh's bed. She wanted only thoughts of their lovemaking and to think about being together with him again that night. But it was impossible to have only happy thoughts with armed militia from Texas camped at the south end of the lake. All along the drive from Forgotten Lake to Duluth, her mood had swung between joy and dread, and now, seated in a Mexican restaurant in Canal Park, her mother was making happy thoughts even more difficult. No sooner had they been seated and placed their order—white wine and taco salad for Diane, enchiladas and beer for Cass—than her mother had launched her verbal barrage.

"And how, pray tell, did militia from Texas find its way to Forgotten Lake?" Diane demanded to know.

Cass shrugged. "Hamilton Madison's apparently the connection."

"No surprise there. That man is dangerous, but your father's never had the good sense to see that. And now something terrible's going to happen, I just know it."

It was a fear Cass shared, but she was loath to agree with her mother. "You might be overstating a bit."

"Overstating? Your father's gone mad, his minions are running amok, and there's armed militia at the lake. No, Cassandra, I'm not overstating, and you've got to get out of there before it all blows up. Come back to Minneapolis with us today."

"All my things are at the lake."

"Well, go get them and then get out of there. I'm serious, Cassandra. Your father's put you in a very dangerous situation."

Cass thought once more of Brian and shook her head. "I'm just not ready to leave yet, Mother." Then to change the subject, she asked, "What sort of business does Gerald have in Duluth today?"

"It's a committee or a commission he serves on. It has something to do with Lake Superior, but I couldn't tell you exactly what." Diane paused for a sip of wine. "He was appointed by the governor."

"How nice."

"Well, it is rather nice, actually. Gerald and the governor are old friends, but it's much more than that. The governor trusts Gerald's judgment, and he often turns to him when he wants something looked into quietly. He's sort of a valued, unofficial emissary."

"Kind of a spy, huh?" Cass said, hoping to needle her mother.

It worked, as Diane bristled. "No, not a spy. A wise and trusted counsel, and you should be so lucky as to have a man in your life with half as much to offer. For that matter, when was the last time you even had a man in your life?"

Now it was Cass's turn to bristle. "What makes you think I don't have a man in my life now?"

Diane raised her eyebrows. "Well, do you?"

Cass nodded, already wishing she hadn't risen to her mother's bait.

"Really? In New Orleans?"

Cass shook her head. "At the lake."

"Dear God! Please don't tell me that you've taken up with one of your father's minions."

"No, he works for the Soil and Water Conservation District."

"How charming," Diane said, her voice heavy with sarcasm.

"He's a civil engineer, and as a matter of fact, he is rather charming."

"A charming engineer. How nice for you."

"Stop it, Mother."

"No, I won't stop it. Between your choice of a career in economics and your taste in men, you seem to have this penchant for the dreary side of life. Come to Minneapolis. Get away from all ... this."

At that moment the thing Cass most wanted to get away from was her mother.

CHAPTER 18

*B*rian Walsh sat at his desk, shuffling papers around without accomplishing much at all. It was late afternoon and he hadn't been able to concentrate all day, as thoughts of Cass and the previous night kept crowding out any attempt at work. No surprise there. A hydrology study was no match for the memory of her soft skin against his own, and if that weren't enough, there were also the plans they'd made for the coming night. Before parting that morning at Brian's cabin, they had agreed to get together after her return from Duluth, and Cass then suggested that he come to Forgotten Lake.

"Jack may not think much of that," Brian cautioned. "I'm not exactly his favorite person."

"It's time for him to get over that," she said. "And if it gets too awkward, we don't have to stay. We can pack a picnic and take the boat over to the island."

"A picnic sounds good."

"And we can swim over there too."

"So ... I should bring trunks?"

Cass had answered with a playful smile and a vague suggestion that he travel light, and with that all hope for the hydrology study was lost. The blossoming relationship with Cass was also new motivation to settle Jack's dam issue once and for all. Brian was confident that could happen, though he was somewhat concerned about the addition of Clancy Meeker to the mix. He had looked into the

wannabe congressman and determined that he was indeed a light-
weight who really did go around in a coonskin cap. His election
seemed unlikely, but he could still complicate matters at Forgotten
Lake. Still, Brian Walsh was falling in love, and with love came
optimism, and optimism told him that Meeker could be dealt with.
Optimism also allowed his thoughts to wander to skinny dipping
with Cass on the island, which was where his thoughts were when
Zack Buchwald walked up to his desk.

"Just got a call from Hank Cross," the office manager said.

Brian tensed. Calls from the sheriff's office seldom conveyed
good news. "Yeah?"

"And Roscoe 'No Sweat' Dugan was there with him."

Definitely not good news, Brian thought.

"Sounds like your pal Baird's up to his old tricks again," Zack said.

"How's that?"

"Well, as Hank described the situation, Roscoe noticed the flow
on the Bumble dropping this afternoon, and he immediately concluded—with good reason, I might add—that Baird had put the
dam in again. Only this time, instead of letting the authorities deal
with it, Roscoe decided to take matters into his own hands, so he
jumped in his car and drove up to Forgotten Lake."

Brian winced at the thought of a direct confrontation between
Dugan and Jack. "So what'd No Sweat find? Is the dam in again?"

Zack shrugged. "Who knows? Roscoe never made it to the lake.
He parked and started up the trail through the woods, but after just
a few yards, he found himself staring down the barrel of a rifle."

"Oh, shit! Was it Jack?"

Zack shook his head. "Roscoe had never seen the guy before.
But get this: he said the guy was all decked out in camo and he had
a sidearm in addition to the rifle. I believe the term Roscoe used to
describe him was paramilitary."

"What happened then?"

"Apparently, the guy with the gun told Roscoe that continuing
on would be a bad idea and that he oughta get his ass off the property.
Well, Roscoe had enough sense not to argue with someone pointing

a rifle at his head, so he cleared outta there and went straight to the sheriff's office. Hank says he's livid, as you might expect."

"So why'd Hank call here?" Brian asked, without really wanting to hear the answer.

"Because our office has been involved with this Forgotten Lake mess from the start. And I guess that means you. Have you seen any paramilitary types when you've been out there?"

"No, and I actually thought, hoped at least, that Jack was losing interest in the dam." Brian thought a moment. "The only development out there lately that I know of is that Clancy Meeker, that goofball running for Congress, has been stirring things up. The guy that ran Dugan off wasn't by any chance wearing a coonskin cap?"

"No," Zack said, "and I know who Meeker is. The guy Roscoe described to Hank didn't sound like Meeker at all. This guy sounded … dangerous. Meeker's just … stupid."

"So what happens next?" Brian asked. "Is Hank taking some people out there?"

"No way. At least not right away. It's like everyone's walking on eggshells. I guess the phone lines between Forsythe and Duluth have been burning up, and the last thing they want is for this thing to escalate any more than it has. When people start mentioning places like Ruby Ridge and Waco in the same breath as Forgotten Lake, you know they're taking it damn seriously."

"Sounds like a standoff," Brian said, as his hopes for skinny dipping at Forgotten Lake that night quickly faded.

"Yeah, I suppose it is a standoff for now," Zack said, "but they're actually looking to get proactive. They're putting together a special team to deal with it. They've got guys coming from the state, from the Bureau of Criminal Apprehension, and also the feds."

"You mean the FBI?"

Zack shrugged. "Yeah, or ATF or one of those other alphabet outfits. The governor's even put a special unit of the National Guard that's trained to deal with terrorism on alert, but that's an absolute last resort, because once those boys are in it, it looks like all-out war."

Brian sighed. "And I thought the whole mess was about to go away."

"No, it's not going away," Zack said, "and you, my friend, are right in the middle of it."

"What's that supposed to mean?"

"It means that you're on the team. That's the main reason Hank called."

"Me? Hell, Zack, I'm not law enforcement. I'm ... I'm an engineer and a bureaucrat. I've got no business on a team like that."

"That's where they disagree," Zack said. "Oh, no one expects you to carry a gun or to be involved in any way should things go bad, but they want your input for background. They're actually going to do some profiling, and they think you can be helpful with that. After all, you've been there from the start."

"I don't care. I don't wanna be on the team."

"You don't have a choice. You're on it. What's more, you're expected at the sheriff's office in half an hour. The team's gathering there and they're planning a pretty extensive work session for tonight. Hope you didn't have any plans."

After Zack left, Brian sat staring glumly at the neglected work on his desk, amazed at how quickly things had changed. He had gone from eager anticipation of skinny dipping with Cass, not to mention other delights, to now facing the unpleasant prospect of spending the evening with a team assembled to deal with paramilitary types at Forgotten Lake. *What the hell is going on out there?* He picked up his cell phone and speed dialed Cass's number, but the screen reported her cell out of service. No surprise there, he thought. She was probably back at the lake where cellular service was nonexistent. He hesitated a moment; then he thought what the hell, he had to know what was going on. He punched in Jack's landline number.

Jack answered gruffly after the third ring. "Yeah?"

"Is Cass there?"

"Who's calling?"

"Brian Walsh."

There was a long pause, during which Brian imagined Jack debating whether to hang up; then Jack said, "Wait a sec."

A moment later, Cass came on the line. "Hello?"

"What's going on out there?"

"Brian ... this isn't a good time to talk."

"When will it be a good time?"

"I'm ... it's hard to say, but definitely not now. And it's probably not a good idea for you to come out here tonight."

"Oh, tonight's already been canceled," he said; then he realized that it wasn't the best time to mention the law enforcement team being assembled to deal with whatever her father was up to. "Something's come up at this end. Looks like I'll be tied up most of the evening."

"Oh, well ..."

"Cass, when can I see you? We need to talk."

"Um, I'm not sure, but soon I hope. And I have to go now. Sorry." With that she broke the connection.

* * *

Cass stared down at the phone for a long moment after hanging up; then she turned to face her father, ready to resume the argument they'd been having since her return from Duluth. Fifteen minutes earlier the argument had grown more intense with the arrival of Hamilton Madison, who sat at the table with a satisfied smirk on his face.

"Dad, you're playing with fire," she said. "You've gotta get those people off your land before it blows up in your face."

Jack grimaced and appeared to waver as he had throughout the argument, but then Ham spoke up. "There's no law against him letting folks camp on his property."

Cass turned angrily to Ham. "Campers, huh? Campers who just happen to be armed to the teeth."

Ham shrugged. "You can't defend the Constitution with slingshots. And every one of those weapons is properly permitted."

"This is ridiculous," Cass said. "Dad's involved in a simple land use dispute, one he happens to be on the losing side of, and you're trying to turn it into a constitutional crisis. This is dangerous and it's gotta stop!"

"You're forgetting that they illegally confiscated Jack's gun in clear violation of his Second Amendment rights."

Cass turned back to her father. "Are you going to listen to this fool, or are you going to listen to reason? You'll get your gun back eventually, and you won't need armed militia to do it."

Jack pondered a moment. "Ham, how many militia types we got down there now?"

"The Idaho boys arrived an hour ago," Ham said. "That brings us to fourteen."

Jack pondered again. "Does seem like a bit more firepower than the situation calls for."

"Now don't you go getting cold feet on me, Jack," Ham said. "These are true patriots, and they've come from all over the country to stand with you, and now you've got a moral duty to stand with them."

"Moral duty!" Cass was incredulous. "How about a moral duty to obey the law? How about a moral duty to avoid recklessly provoking armed men?"

"Enough, already!" Jack held up his hand; then he turned to Ham. "Cass has a point. Things may be getting a little outta hand and—"

"Damn it, Jack," Ham protested. "These men are committed, and it's not the kind of commitment that can be taken lightly."

"They may be committed, but I still got the last word. Major Mike said so himself. Now here's what's gonna happen," Jack said, pointing at Ham. "First thing tomorrow, you and me are gonna go down there and get a few things straight. We'll go in my boat so we won't have to mess with their goddamn picket line, and we'll—"

"Just exactly what is it you wanna get straight?" Ham asked.

"Well, for starters, I don't want any goddamn wars starting on my property."

Ham started to protest again but Jack cut him off. "That's the way it's gonna be." He gave a nod of finality, first to Ham, then to Cass, neither of whom looked happy.

CHAPTER 19

*T*he sun had just set and Jack Baird stood at the end of his dock, casting a line into the still water. He liked to fish at sunset. Walleyes often came into shallower water with the fading light to feed, but even when they weren't biting it was a good time to be alone with his thoughts. And this evening his thoughts were troubled and in need of sorting out. Now he slowly reeled the line in, feeling for the sudden tug of a fish hitting his bait, but none came, and when he had drawn the minnow up to the dock, he looked down to ensure that it was still swimming; then he cast it out again. A loon called across the lake. It was a sound Jack had delighted in all his life, a sound that was both melodic and peaceful, but on this night his ear seemed to detect a different tone, one more haunting than peaceful, a warning of trouble ahead.

Jack gave a rueful chuckle. There was indeed a chance of trouble ahead. Cass was right. Things were threatening to get out of hand, and it had all started so innocently with a simple desire to avoid denting his boat. That had led to the dam, and the dam had led to a helluva mess. Jack knew he was responsible for much of the mess, but others were at fault too. Certainly, things would have gone differently had not that asshole deputy shot at him. Hamilton Madison wasn't helping either, though Jack probably should have reined him in sooner. He looked down the lake to the south end where the glow of a bonfire and several lanterns marked the militia's campsite. Yes,

things were definitely getting out of hand, but the thing that bothered Jack most was Cass's strong objection. She, more than anyone,
had always taken his side over matters at Forgotten Lake. She loved
it there as much as he, but now she seemed to be choosing the other
side. An hour earlier she had brusquely announced that she was
going out. When Jack asked where she was going she had glared a
moment, then simply said, "Out," and walked away. Moments later
he heard her car drive off, leaving him to wonder if she was going
to see Brian Walsh and if he might not see her until morning again.
She could do that if she wanted—she was an adult, after all—but it
was the thought of losing her to the other side that now made him
want to dig his heels in deeper.

The sound of an outboard motor interrupted his thoughts and
he looked up to see a boat coming in through the fading light. It
was Dup Dingle. Dup slowed as he got close, then cut the motor
and glided in to bump against the dock. He wrapped a mooring
line around a dock post, but remained seated rather than climbing
from the boat.

"Hey, Jack."

"Hey, Dup."

"Catching anything?"

"Nope."

Dup paused a moment; then he pointed toward the campfire
and lantern lights at the south end of the lake. "Some deal, huh?"

"Yup."

Dup pondered as he continued looking toward the lights. "How
long you reckon them militia fellas gonna be here?"

Jack shrugged. "Not sure. Why, you got a problem with them?"

"Well, they're sure as hell making me all nervous. We never had
no militia around here before, and I can't say I like having 'em now."

"I don't think they'll bother you any."

"So you say, but it seems to me with all them guns everywhere
things could get outta kilter mighty damn quick."

There it was, Jack thought. Even Dup Dingle was taking the
other side. What was the point in having minions if you couldn't

count on them? Actually, he was beginning to wonder if Hamilton Madison and the militia were really on his side, if they might not have agendas of their own. "It'll all work out, Dup. We gotta get a few things ironed out, and then the militia can be on their way."

"I sure hope so," Dup said. "It's getting so I can hardly sleep at night."

The loon called again, its haunting tone a reminder that trouble was, indeed, still close at hand.

* * *

It was after ten that night when Brian Walsh finally left the sheriff's office in Forsythe and walked out to his pickup. The team's work session had lasted five hours and his stomach now churned from the pizza and coffee they had consumed while they worked. His head ached too, but that he attributed to the tension rising from the team's makeup and mission.

A pecking order had been established early on and it was soon apparent that Brian was of the lowest order. That was fine with him. He had no desire to play a prominent role on the team, but after five hours he did feel rather pecked over. Most of the pecking had come early, as he was grilled at length about every last detail he could recall about Jack Baird and the events at Forgotten Lake. Mere facts weren't enough. They also wanted to understand the mindset of everyone involved. When it finally became clear that Brian had no knowledge of armed men at Forgotten Lake, they turned their attention elsewhere, leaving him to look on and eat pizza.

Next above Brian in the pecking order was Deputy Sam Skinner, chosen for the team because he was a competent officer and also because, like Brian, he'd been involved with Jack Baird and his dam. Then came Hank Cross, the supervising deputy in the Forsythe sheriff's office, followed by Stan Green, an assistant county attorney who'd driven up from Duluth. Representing the state of Minnesota was Agent Mitch White, of the Bureau of Criminal Apprehension, and for the feds an agent named Andy Black, of Alcohol, Tobacco and Firearms. Both Black and White stressed the need for inter-agency cooperation, though each seemed mindful of his respective turf, and when disputes arose it was usually Black of ATF who asserted the fed prerogative.

It had quickly occurred to Brian that, between Black and White and Green, the team's leadership was conveniently color coded by jurisdiction. Then as the evening wore on, he assigned to himself the color blue as a good fit for his darkening mood, a mood that wasn't helped by the presence of Commissioner Roscoe "No Sweat" Dugan. Dugan wasn't officially part of the team, but as a locally elected official with ties to the Forgotten Lake affair, he insisted on sitting in. Black and White tried to tolerate him, but that tolerance was soon strained. Dugan started off by demanding a press conference so that the world would know that Commissioner Dugan had been threatened at gunpoint in the performance of his duties.

"Not a good idea," said Black of ATF.

"But the public has a right to know about a threat like this in their midst," Dugan countered.

"The public will be informed in due course," said White of BCA, "but so far the media are largely unaware of the scope of things at Forgotten Lake and for now it's best to keep it that way."

"We're at a sensitive stage," said Black. "We need to open communication lines with these people, and involving the press now will only hinder that."

"Communication lines, huh?" Dugan sneered. "How 'bout opening some firing lines. Go in there and clean 'em out."

"Really bad idea, Commissioner," said White.

"Our number one goal is to avoid escalating the situation and inadvertently setting off a powder keg," said Green.

Dugan whined a bit more until Black and White ran out of patience and made it clear to the commissioner that he could be quiet and eat pizza or leave the meeting. Given that choice Dugan finally shut up, though in protest he refused the pizza and glowered silently instead.

Eventually, after hours of speculation and conjecture, the team arrived at a plan. The first step was to make contact without provoking an incident. It was deemed best to do that through Jack Baird, as they all agreed that the worst thing they could do was just show up with a show of force. Jack could presumably provide vital intelligence, such as how many men were actually there, how extensively they were armed, and what was motivating them. Hopefully Jack would then facilitate contact with the armed men, which was the sensitive next step in defusing the situation. In assessing Jack, the gathered experts had arrived at a profile that boiled down to "grumpy contrarian," and given that they again ruled out a show of force in approaching him. Rather, a small, less threatening team would make the initial contact with Jack. That team would consist of Agent Black of ATF, because Agent Black said so, and Hank Cross, because he represented local law enforcement and was known to Jack. Black and White then agreed that the third and final member of the Jack Baird contact team would be, to the dismay of Brian Walsh, Brian Walsh.

"But Jack doesn't like me," Brian protested. "He blames me for most of his trouble. Sending me in there won't do much to gain his cooperation."

"But he knows you," said Black. "That's important. We don't want him to feel as if he's being bombarded with a lot of new unknowns."

"Even if you're not a favorite," said Green, "you don't present a new threat. That's what we want to avoid: the perception of a growing threat level."

"Exactly," said White. "A calm, steady state is what we want."

In the end, they agreed that the team would drive to Jack Baird's home on Forgotten Lake the next morning, arriving in Hank Cross's cruiser to lend an official air. More deputies and cruisers would be staged nearby, but out of sight, should a need for assistance arise. Hopefully Jack would cooperate and they would proceed from there. At the suggestion of Deputy Sam Skinner, the team would come bearing doughnuts as a show of goodwill that might resonate with Jack.

"What about the National Guard?" Roscoe Dugan asked, breaking his imposed silence.

"What about 'em?" said Black.

"It's my understanding that the governor has ordered a special antiterrorist unit on alert. I think they should be here and standing by, ready to move in."

Black and White could only shake their heads.

And now Brian climbed into his pickup, his head aching, his stomach churning, dreading the coming day. The night had cooled and as he drove to his cabin he rolled down the window, filling the cab with pine-scented air. It was a scent that usually invigorated him, but this night it did nothing for his dark mood. When he reached his cabin, though, his headache and churning stomach were quickly forgotten, his mood lifting at the sight of the car parked there, Cass's car.

* * *

"Militia from Texas and Idaho?" Brian shook his head in disbelief. "This is ... just plain nuts!"

Cass could only shrug.

"Any idea how many?" he asked.

"Fourteen according to Hamilton Madison," Cass said. They were seated on the couch in Brian's living room, each with a glass of scotch on the rocks.

"And who's Hamilton Madison again?"

"The local conspiracy nut," she said. "He's got a cabin across the lake from Dad's place. He and Dup Dingle make up what my mother calls Dad's minions. Dup's pretty harmless, but Ham's got some strange ideas and apparently connections to go with them. He was the one who contacted the militia in the first place."

"Armed militia." He shook his head again. "I was afraid it would turn out to be something like that."

She gave him a quizzical look. "What do you mean, you were afraid? Did you already know something about it?"

"Yeah." He related how Roscoe Dugan had gone to Forgotten Lake because the Bumble was dropping again, only to be run off at gunpoint by a man dressed in camo, and that Dugan had then gone straight to the sheriff's office.

"So the authorities know." She sighed and paused for a gulp of scotch. "What's going to happen now?"

"Well, they're taking it damn seriously," he said. "They don't want another Ruby Ridge or Waco." He went on to describe the team that had been assembled to deal with Forgotten Lake.

"Dear God! BCA *and* ATF?" Now it was Cass who shook her head. "Dad, what've you done?"

"It gets worse."

"How can it?"

"I'm on the team."

"No, Brian! Why, for God's sake?"

He shrugged. "Because I've been involved. They think I can help with background stuff. Believe me, it wasn't my idea. I basically got dragooned into it."

"So what's next?"

"Tomorrow morning your dad'll have some visitors." Brian then related how he and Agent Black and Hank Cross would approach Jack and seek his help in opening lines of communication with the militiamen.

"Good luck with that," she said.

"You don't think he'll be willing to help?"

She shrugged. "I just don't know, Brian. At times I think he listens to me and starts to waver, but then Hamilton Madison comes along and gets him all stoked up again. And when he gets something in his head, he can get awfully stubborn, and then he's even less likely to listen to reason."

Brian put down his drink and slid his arm around her shoulders. "I hope this doesn't, um ... affect us."

She offered a weak smile. "I hope so too, but everything feels like it's on hold until this god-awful business gets resolved."

He paused before asking, "Can you stay tonight?"

"I … I should get back to the lake."

"You're at a lake."

"You know what I mean," she said. "With everything happening tomorrow morning, I should be there."

"Will you tell him?" he asked. "About the team?"

"Probably. I don't know. It doesn't feel right to hold it back, and he'll find out anyway when you show up tomorrow."

"I wish you'd stay."

She leaned in and kissed him on the lips. "Can't." And then she was gone.

* * *

Hamilton Madison sat in the Adirondack chair in front of his cabin, drinking his nightly bourbon on the rocks—his third actually. Three bourbons usually make him rather mellow, but this night the booze was stoking a brooding anger. He looked down the lake to the south end where a bonfire flickered in the militia's campsite. A lot of good men down there, he thought, everyone a true patriot, and some mighty fine women too. He smiled at the thought of Wanda's tits and knocked back a gulp of bourbon. Yes, good men and women who had traveled a long way to defend the Constitution and fight the government's treachery, and now it might all go for naught because Jack Baird was getting cold feet. Oh, Jack claimed otherwise, but Ham knew better. Just that afternoon the old man had wavered in his commitment to the militia all because of his damn daughter's bleeding heart whining. If Ham hadn't been there to counter her arguments, she'd probably have gotten away with it. What they didn't understand, what Hamilton Madison understood only too well, is that when the government violates the Constitution there is a moral duty to resist.

Ham doubted that any good would come from going with Jack the next morning to meet with the militia and, as Jack put it, get a few things straight. The old man was just looking for a way to weasel out, but Ham wasn't about to let that happen. No, sir! Maybe he wouldn't show up at Jack's house in the morning. Maybe he'd go straight to the militia campsite instead. Maybe it was time to stop trusting old men with cold feet and seize the day, especially now that the militia was here. It would be a crime to let the government's treachery go unchecked when true patriots were on hand to resist. Steeled with new resolve, Hamilton Madison knocked back the last of his bourbon, then stood and walked to his cabin. Time for bed. Tomorrow promised to be a big day.

CHAPTER 20

$\mathcal{T}$he box of doughnuts sat unopened in the middle of the table, an intended goodwill gesture that had become a metaphor for the tension in the room. Jack and Cass Baird sat on one side of the table facing Agent Black of ATF, Deputy Hank Cross, and Brian Walsh on the other. The fifteen minutes since the negotiating team's arrival had been characterized by terse comments punctuated by awkward silences with Cass and Brian stealing brief glances at each other.

Now, after a particularly long silence, Agent Black tried to start anew. He turned to look out the front of the house at Forgotten Lake; then he faced Jack again and said, "Peaceful place you have here, Mr. Baird."

Jack's only response was a grunt.

"Please understand," Black continued, "that our greatest desire is that it stays peaceful. We didn't come here looking for a fight."

"You think I am?" said Jack. "All I want is for people to mind their own business and leave me alone."

"And we respect that," Black said. "But we do have a situation here. Having armed militia on your property is not conducive to keeping the peace, and we'd very much appreciate your help in cooling things off."

Jack shrugged. "You fellas got the law and everything on your side. Don't know why you need me."

"We need you to help us make contact. Once contact is made, we can begin a serious conversation and negotiations with them, but the moment of initial contact is critical. It's a moment when misunderstandings can lead to unintended violence. We think you can help us with that."

Jack glowered in silence for several uncomfortable moments. Finally, Black asked, "So, Mr. Baird, will you help us?"

Again silence from Jack; then Cass spoke. "If he won't, I will."

Jack looked at his daughter, surprised. "How you gonna do that? The militia don't even know you."

"No, but Hamilton Madison does."

"Who's Hamilton Madison?" asked Black

"A fella that lives across the lake," Jack said.

"He's a conspiracy nut," Cass said. "He's the one responsible for the militia being here."

Black looked at Jack. "Is that right, Mr. Baird?"

Jack shrugged. "I suppose. He was supposed to be here this morning, but he never showed up."

"That's because he's probably down there with the militia." Cass looked across the table to Black. "My offer to help with making contact stands."

Jack shook his head. "Aw, what the hell, I'll help you, but I've got some conditions."

Black nodded and leaned forward. "Let's hear them."

"First, I get my gun back."

Black turned to Hank Cross who said, "I talked to the county attorney in Duluth this morning. You'll have your gun by this afternoon."

Jack gave a nod of approval. "And second, the dam stays."

Black turned to Brian now. "Would you address that, Mr. Walsh?"

After a quick glance at Cass, Brian said, "Well, I can't give you an answer by this afternoon, but here's what I can do. You have a right to apply for a permit for the dam. If you choose to do so, I will personally assist you in making the application, as the process gets rather technical. Furthermore, I'm already on record with my office as recommending that the dam be approved based on its technical and environmental merits, and I will make that recommendation as a formal appendix to your application. Understand that I can't guarantee the outcome, but I'd say the chances are good. That's the best we can do for now."

All eyes turned to Jack and Black said, "Well, Mr. Baird?"

After a moment Jack said, "Seems like you fellas kinda anticipated what I'd want."

"We want to work with you," Black said.

Jack turned to his daughter who gave him an encouraging nod; then he looked across the table again. "What the hell, how you wanna go about it?"

* * *

"We can't count on him anymore," said Hamilton Madison. "He's getting cold feet."

"You sure?" Major Mike asked.

Ham had arrived at the militia's campsite minutes earlier and now he was seated by the campfire with Major Mike and Wanda. Each held a mug of coffee, but after hearing Ham's news they seemed to have lost interest in drinking it. "Yeah, I'm sure," Ham said. "Jack don't really care about the Constitution. When it gets down to it, he's just an old man who wants to go fishing."

"Well, that throws a wrench into the works," Major Mike said. "Hell, he's the property owner. It'll be tough to carry on the mission without his support."

"But you can't leave," Ham said. "Not now. There's too much at stake. We can't let the government stomp all over the Constitution just because some old fart loses his nerve."

They lapsed into dejected silence and after a moment, Ham nodded toward the newly completed dam. "By the way," he said, "the dam looks really good."

"Yeah, the guys did a good job. Be a shame to see the effort go for nothing." Major Mike pondered a moment. "Do you suppose it'd help if I talked to Jack?"

"That's exactly what I'm thinking," Ham said. "In fact, Jack's coming here this morning, any minute now. That's why I came ahead, so we could work out a strategy for dealing with him. He needs some new inspiration and I figure you're just the man to give it to him."

"If he's coming, I'd better let the sentries know." Major Mike picked up a walkie-talkie, then turned to Wanda. "Who's out on picket this morning?"

"Zeke and Mack," she said.

Major Mike keyed the radio and spoke into it, and a moment later Zeke responded. Major Mike then instructed him to expect a visit from Jack Baird and to escort him into camp when he arrived. Major Mike put the radio down, gave a nod of satisfaction to Wanda, and said, "Good thing we brought the walkie-talkies. The cell service around here sucks."

"Yeah, and that's part of another government conspiracy," Ham said, "but now we gotta figure out how to get Jack back on track."

"So what's he objecting to?" Major Mike asked. "What's his bitch?"

"Oh, he's got this smart-ass daughter who keeps nagging him about obeying the law and keeping outta trouble. She gets him all hung up with petty stuff and he loses sight of the big picture—that when the government violates the Constitution, then folks like us have a duty to go *looking* for trouble."

Major Mike pondered a moment; then Wanda spoke. "Nullification. That's the angle we oughta take."

Both men turned to look at her, with Ham's eyes automatically drawn to her breasts, which were once more swelling gloriously from her camo top. "Yeah," said Major Mike, "good call, Wanda. Nullification just might be the ticket that brings Jack's thinking around."

"Nullification?" Ham looked confused. "What's that supposed to mean?"

"It's actually a legal theory," Major Mike said. "It holds that a state can nullify or invalidate federal laws that are deemed unconstitutional. Nullification empowers states when the government oversteps its bounds, and Wanda's point is that the same kind of empowerment can be extended to individuals."

"So how would that work with Jack?" Ham asked.

"Well, the government has clearly violated his Second Amendment rights, so under nullification he gets his gun back. And since they're trampling all over his property rights on the dam thing, he probably wins there too."

Ham's eyebrows knitted as he worked through it. "What happens if the government tries to, um ... nullify the nullification?"

Major Mike shrugged. "That just forces the next step."

"Which is?"

Major Mike paused to look at Wanda, who smiled and nodded; then he turned back to Ham. "Which is secession."

"Secession! Really?" Ham looked incredulous. "Seems like you folks in Texas are always talking about seceding, but you never do it."

"Don't ... bet ... against it!" Wanda spat the words. "It's gonna happen, and it's gonna happen a lot sooner than people think."

Ham was briefly taken aback by Wanda's vehemence. "Don't get me wrong," he said, "I hope it does happen, but a state seceding is a bit different than the situation here."

"Why should it be?" Major Mike said. "If a state can secede under the theory of nullification, then why's it any different for a lake if the government's acting unconstitutionally?"

Ham thought a moment; then a smile slowly spread across his face. "I like it," he nodded. "I like it a lot. Yeah! This country could stand a helluva lot more thinking like that." He raised his coffee mug. "I'll even drink to it: to the Forgotten Lake secession!"

They all raised their mugs just as Zeke's voice crackled over the walkie-talkie. Major Mike picked up the radio and keyed it. "Yeah, Zeke, is Jack there?"

Zeke's voice came back. "Looks like it, but he's got a bunch of company with him. I count two cop cars and a pickup. We got armed men standing on the road."

"Shit!" said Ham. "That fucking traitor!"

Major Mike thought a moment, then keyed the radio again. "Don't engage them, Zeke. Repeat, don't engage them. We're going into defense posture, plan A. We'll be taking up positions the way we discussed, so be aware of where everyone is. We don't want casualties from friendly fire. And remember, this is a defensive posture. We don't shoot first."

Major Mike put down the radio, stood, and picked up his semi-automatic rifle; then he called out to the others in camp. "Everybody arm up! We've got company and we're going into defensive plan A. Go to your assigned positions and keep out of sight."

"And remember," shouted Wanda, "God is with you!"

A shiver went down Hamilton Madison's spine. It was a glorious moment. True patriots were standing against tyranny.

* * *

With Jack Baird having agreed to help with contacting the militia, Agent Black of ATF and Deputy Hank Cross determined that an enhanced presence would be appropriate for the next step. A radio call was made and soon they were joined by another cruiser driven by Deputy Sam Skinner with White of BCA and Assistant County Attorney Green on board. The two cruisers then proceeded to the south end of the lake with Black, Cross, and Brian Walsh in the lead car. They were followed by Jack Baird in his pickup. Jack had intended to go alone, but Cass had insisted on accompanying him, and Jack had been unable to dissuade her.

Upon reaching the Bumble River, they parked by the side of the road and climbed from their vehicles. The two deputies were in uniform, complete with sidearms. Black and White wore dark blue windbreakers with their respective agency initials in large white letters on the back. They, too, had donned sidearms. Black and White and the deputies then huddled with Jack at the side of the road, with Green and Brian and Cass looking on a few yards away.

"They're sure to have sentries posted, so they already know we're here," Black said. "Mr. Baird, I think it's best that they hear from you first." He held out the battery-powered megaphone he'd been carrying.

Jack recoiled from the megaphone. "Me? I don't know what the hell to say to 'em."

"Start by identifying yourself," Black said, "then ask if one or two of them will come out to talk. Emphasize that we only want to talk, to understand their position."

Jack looked decidedly unhappy, but he reluctantly took the megaphone from Black. "So how do you work this contraption?"

"Just press this key, then raise it to your mouth, and speak."

Jack shook his head, then raised the megaphone to his mouth but before he could speak, strains of music suddenly sounded through the air. Everyone looked around to see where the music was coming from, and as they did the music grew louder.

"What the hell?" Black said, pointing. "It's coming from up the road."

They all looked up the road as the music grew louder still, but its source remained a mystery. "Isn't that the army song?" Sam Skinner asked.

"Yeah," White said. "'And Those Caissons Go Rolling Along.'"

At that moment a pickup appeared, cresting a rise in the road a hundred yards away. The music seemed to be coming from a pair of speakers mounted on the roof of its cab and a man stood in the pickup's box, waving his arm. In the next moment another vehicle appeared behind the pickup, a bus, and then a second bus, followed by what looked like two TV sound trucks. The lead pickup was closer now, fifty yards away, and they could see that the man in the pickup's box was wearing a coonskin cap and, to everyone's horror, that he wasn't just waving his arm. He was waving a shotgun.

"What the fuck?" said Black.

"Aw, shit," said Jack. "I forgot all about him."

Black turned to Jack. "You know that guy?"

"He's some goddamn politician."

"Well, what the hell's he doing here?" Black demanded.

Jack could only shrug as the pickup came to a stop fifty feet away, just as the caissons stopped rolling along. For a brief moment silence hung in the air; then "Anchors Aweigh" blared from the speakers as people began pouring from the buses.

* * *

Major Mike keyed the walkie-talkie. "What the hell's going on, Zeke? I can't see the road from my position. What's with the music?"

Zeke's voice crackled over the radio. "Beats the shit outta me. The music could be a diversion. All I know for sure is that it's getting damn crowded. They're coming in on buses now. There's people all over the place."

"Are they armed," Major Mike asked.

"Hard to say," Zeke came back. "But some are for sure. You suppose they're fixing to attack? Can't think of another reason they'd need so many."

"I don't know," Major Mike said. "Keep low for now. Don't give your position away. Let's see what their next move is." He put the radio down and turned to Wanda. They had set up their command post behind a fallen tree halfway between the lake and the road with the rest of the militia spread in similar positions throughout the area. "This might be it," he said. "This might be the big one we've been training for."

Wanda nodded, the tip of her tongue flicking across her upper lip as she reached with her hand to caress the barrel of her semiautomatic rifle.

* * *

Agent Black of ATF stormed up to the pickup. "Turn off that goddamn music and get those people back on those buses!"

Clancy Meeker shouted over the music. "This here music is speech, and those people are assembling peacefully. It's all protected by the First Amendment and you got no business trying to stop it."

"The hell I don't!" Black held up his badge. "You're interfering with a law enforcement operation. And put that gun down!"

"Now you're violating the Second Amendment," Clancy yelled and raised the shotgun higher still as two men with shoulder-mounted TV cameras began taping.

Standing up the road, Cass turned to Brian. "This is just nuts. It can't possibly get any crazier."

And then it did.

Agent Black, still yelling to make himself heard over "Anchors Aweigh," shouted, "I'm not going to tell you again. Put down that gun!"

Clancy shouted, "No way! You already took a man's gun away out here once, and it ain't gonna happen again." He did a quarter turn so that he faced the TV cameras. "This here rally is in support of the Second Amendment, and I will now salute the Second Amendment the only way the Second Amendment oughta be saluted." With that he fired the shotgun into the air.

* * *

Major Mike keyed the walkie-talkie. "Who fired that shot, Zeke? Them or us?"

"I think it was them," Zeke said. "Kinda hard to tell though. Things are getting pretty crazy. You want we should return fire?"

Before Major Mike could reply, two of the militiamen did open fire and over the next few seconds shots rang out everywhere.

* * *

Total chaos reigned on the road. People were running everywhere, diving into roadside ditches, trying to cram back on the buses. Clancy Meeker gaped about in open-mouth wonder until a bullet found his left buttock. The impact flipped him out of the pickup and onto the gravel road where he thrashed about and screamed, "I'm hit! I'm hit!"

Cass and Brian had dived into the ditch on the side of the road away from the shooting. A moment later Jack tumbled into the same ditch ten feet away.

"Dad, are you alright?" Cass asked.

"I ain't shot, if that's what you mean, but this business ain't going so good." He peeked over the edge of the road to where Clancy Meeker was still flopping around and hollering; then he ducked down again. "I only wanted to keep from denting my damn boat. That's all I ever wanted!"

CHAPTER 21

$\mathcal{B}$rian Walsh was numb. It had been a long, wearisome day; a day in which he'd been caught up in tense negotiations; a day in which he'd been shot at; and now finally a day in which he'd endured an hour-long media circus. It was late afternoon and the press conference, held in the Forsythe City Council chambers to accommodate the large number of reporters, had just concluded. The TV cameras were packed away and most of the reporters had filed from the room, though a few remained behind, pestering officials with questions that in Brian's view had already been asked and answered several times. Brian himself had been ordered to the conference so that he could answer any questions the media might have regarding the Soil and Water Conservation District's role in the day's events. There had been none, the media being more interested in armed militia and shootouts at Forgotten Lake than environmental matters. Brian was thankful for the lack of questions, and he had been content to observe the conference quietly from the end of the council dais.

The conference had begun with statements from Black of ATF and St. Louis County Sheriff Harrison Brown—another leader, yet another color code, thought Brian—who had driven up from Duluth to take charge of the county's involvement. Both men praised the restraint and professionalism displayed by law enforcement personnel that day at Forgotten Lake. Both men expressed thankfulness that there had been no loss of life. Most of the injuries had been minor, resulting from dives into ditches and stampeding crowds. Miraculously, the only bullet wound had been sustained by Clancy Meeker, and his wound was not deemed life threatening.

Black then described the current deployment of law enforcement personnel at Forgotten Lake. Additional deputies had come up from Duluth to augment the Forsythe staff, and several more ATF agents were now on hand. Deputies and agents were now manning roadblocks on the approaches to the south end of the lake to monitor militia activity and facilitate communication should the militia choose to begin talks. Direct confrontation was to be avoided and a renewed attempt to open a dialogue with the militia would be undertaken the next morning.

Sheriff Brown further reported that the governor of Minnesota had ordered a special antiterror unit of the Minnesota National Guard, a unit that had previously been placed on alert, to proceed to the Forgotten Lake area. Brown emphasized that there were no current plans for the Guard unit to engage the militia. They were only being moved into place as a prudent contingency.

Then, before the conference was opened to questions, the podium was given over to Commissioner Roscoe Dugan for a brief statement, one that proved to be anything but brief. With beads of sweat on his bald head glistening in the bright TV lights, Dugan droned on and on with praise for seemingly every person involved in county government—that is, every person except those working for the Soil and Water Conservation District. He then offered contorted leaps of logic intended to show that his leadership was in large part responsible for all the praiseworthy activity, before concluding by imploring trout fishermen everywhere to join the battle against the terroristic assault threatening their beloved sport.

Deputy Sam Skinner now broke away from a group of deputies and walked over to where Brian sat. "Some crazy deal, huh?" he said.

Brian nodded. "Crazier by the minute."

Sam shook his head. "I keep thinking that none of this would've happened if I hadn't gotten that damn toothache."

Brian shrugged. "Don't beat yourself up. It's not your fault. Who knew things would get so outta hand?"

Agent Black joined them now. He nodded to Sam, then turned to Brian. "Walsh, I guess you can consider yourself off the team. It's a different situation now, a different mission, so we won't be needing you anymore, but I do appreciate your help."

"I don't know that I was much help," Brian said. "I'm just glad no one got killed out there today."

"As we all are," said Black; then he shook his head. "It's a horrible thing to say, but if anyone deserved to get shot, it was that clown in the coonskin cap."

"Yeah," said Brian, "and the sad thing is, he'll probably wind up getting more publicity outta this than he ever hoped for."

"And then some," Black said. "The NRA just released a statement endorsing him for Congress. They're calling him an American hero out of the mold of Davy Crockett."

Sam Skinner shook his head. "That ain't right."

Black shrugged. "It happens. A guy does something totally stupid, gets himself shot in the ass, and they turn him into a goddamn hero."

"Only in America," said Sam.

They all nodded their agreement; then Brian stood and excused himself. Outside of City Hall he paused beside his pickup, pondering what to do next. It was after five, so there was no point in going back to the office. He thought about simply going home to his cabin on Round Lake, but he knew home would be a lonely place that night, and he really didn't want to be alone. To hell with it, he thought; then he climbed into his pickup and headed for Forgotten Lake.

* * *

Hamilton Madison sat in the Adirondack chair in front of his cabin drinking his nightly bourbon on the rocks. The booze usually relaxed him, mellowed him out; other times it gave him clarity of thought to understand conspiratorial subtleties, but this night he needed the bourbon to relieve his mortification.

Ham often fantasized about how he would perform under fire, about standing with true patriots against government tyranny. He usually saw himself fearlessly leading the fight. He would invariably claim victory, though often streaked with blood and sweat, and women would then be drawn to him, women like Wanda, to dress his wounds and lick the sweat from his skin. Yes, Hamilton Madison had imagined many heroic outcomes, but never had he imagined that when the time actually came he would shit his pants.

When Major Mike deployed the militia, Ham had gone into the woods with them. He hadn't brought his rifle that morning—he hadn't anticipated Jack Baird's perfidy—but he did have his sidearm strapped around his waist, so he was ready for action. Major Mike directed him to go with two of the Idaho militiamen, and they took up a position behind a low rock ridge some forty yards from the road. From where they were they couldn't see the road clearly, but they heard the growing racket—the blaring music and the sound of multiple vehicles and much shouting. Ham was unnerved by all the noise and by not being able to see its source. Then a shot rang out. The Idaho militiamen responded by opening fire, shooting blindly toward the road. In the next moment bullets whizzed through the air all around them and Hamilton Madison responded by shitting his pants.

Screaming over the walkie-talkie, Major Mike ordered a cease-fire and after a few terrifying moments the shooting stopped. The sound of departing vehicles came from the road and Major Mike reset the picket line and ordered everyone else to the campsite. Ham had trudged numbly back and gathered with the others near the campfire, and only then did he notice the stink rising from his own pants. Mortified, he hoped others wouldn't notice, but then Wanda sniffed the air and her gaze fell on Ham. She didn't say anything, but the look on her face was not the look of a woman who wanted to lick the sweat from his skin.

Now the bourbon, his third, was finally easing his humiliation, but he knew that it wouldn't last, that tomorrow he'd be sober and still in need of redemption. But how was he to redeem himself? How could he earn the right to again stand among battle-tested true patriots, men who'd never been betrayed by their own bowels? The bourbon gave him sudden insight: Jack Baird was the key. It had been Jack Baird's treachery that led to that day's firefight, and Jack Baird must now atone for that treachery. Major Mike and the militia were stymied. They held a strong defensive position, they could hold off an attack from a much larger force, but they were in no position to take the fight to the enemy. The government could simply wait them out until they ran out of food and supplies. Time was on the government's side, but what Ham saw clearly now was that the dynamics would change dramatically with a Forgotten Lake secession. And secession couldn't happen without the cooperation of the property owner: Jack Baird. For all its strengths, the militia still held no sway over Jack, but Hamilton Madison did. If Ham could convince Jack to secede, then Ham would be redeemed in the eyes of the militia as the one who blazed a path forward. The Forgotten Lake secession would be seen as a new birth of freedom, forged in the manner of his namesakes, Hamilton and Madison, the original architects of American freedom. Yes, Ham nodded, tomorrow he would convince Jack to secede, one way or another. He patted the pistol still strapped to his waist. One way or another.

* * *

Brian lay on his back on a blanket spread over a soft bed of pine needles. Cass straddled him, her breasts swaying with the rhythmic downward grinding of her hips, his own hips rising to meet her as they strained toward climax. Afterward, she sank onto his chest with a sigh, and Brian, looking up through the tree limbs at the first stars of night, gave his own sigh of contentment. It had come a day later than he had anticipated, but he had realized his fantasy of skinny dipping, and more, with Cass.

Earlier he'd had to drive several miles out of his way to avoid the roadblocks at the south end of the lake, and he arrived at the Baird place filled with uncertainty over how he would be received. He wasn't surprised when Jack Baird didn't greet him as he might a long-lost son, but for the first time the open hostility was gone. Something else was missing too: Jack's usual bravado. He seemed worn down, the day's events having taken the fight out of him. He sat on the deck, sipping scotch and staring glumly at the lake, not bothering to wander down to the dock and cast a line in as he did most evenings. But Cass, to Brian's delight, greeted him with a welcoming smile and a warm embrace. Some awkward minutes followed during which he tried to converse with Jack, and when it became apparent that he was in no mood for conversation, Cass announced that she and Brian were taking the boat to the island for a picnic. Jack responded with an indifferent shrug, and Cass then assembled a quick picnic consisting of a bottle of wine and ham and cucumber sandwiches made with crusty rolls.

They landed the boat on a small patch of sand and carried their supplies a few feet into the privacy of the woods where Cass spread the blanket. Brian, unsure of Forgotten Lake picnic protocol, hesitated and asked, "So, um, so do we eat now?"

"Only if you want to," she said with a laugh and started peeling her clothes off. "I'm up for a swim."

As it turned out, swimming was deferred too. Once naked, they kissed and embraced, their embrace growing more ardent until the blanket beckoned. They eventually made it into the water to frolic and splash, but soon the blanket beckoned again.

Now Cass rolled off of him and lay on her side, her head propped up on her hand. He turned to face her, his hand reaching for her hip. "Can we eat now?" he asked.

"Is food all you think about?"

"No, but I have sorta worked up an appetite."

"Yeah, I noticed that." She sat up and reached for the cooler and soon they were eating sandwiches and drinking wine from plastic cups. "So, are you happy now?" she asked.

"Oh, yeah. I've always liked a picnic, but until now I'd never realized how much more fun naked picnicking could be. I could learn to love this island."

"Island nudity is something of a family tradition. My Grandpa Floyd once even contemplated a resort for nudists here." She laughed. "Maybe that's what I should do now, start a nudist colony."

"Januarys will probably be slow."

She waved a dismissive hand. "So, it'll be a seasonal thing. And I could combine it with seminars on economics. Sell it as a sensual and cerebral experience rolled into one. There's gotta be a market for something like that."

"And you'd lead these seminars ... naked?"

She shrugged. "Economics can be pretty dry, you know. A little titillation never hurts."

He reached for her breast. "Speaking of titillation ..."

She slapped his hand away. "There'll be none of that in my seminars."

"Actually, I think I prefer my nudist gatherings to be limited to two, as in you and me. And I can skip the seminars too."

"Now you're thinking small. Be bold. Seize the day. And you gotta admit, it'd be better having nudists around here than militia."

Cass's mention of the militia came like a wet blanket, putting a sudden stop to their playful banter. After some moments of silence, she turned and craned her neck to look down the lake to where the militia's campfire glowed in the night. "I'll sure be glad when they're gone," she said.

"You and everyone else."

"So, what do you think'll happen?" she asked.

He shrugged. "Hopefully cooler heads will prevail. Between the feds and the BCA they've got some people with experience dealing with this sort of thing, good negotiators, and as long as that idiot in the coonskin cap doesn't show up again, they should be able to defuse things. It helps that your dad finally seems to have found his way to the right side. I think today must've been kinda tough on him."

"He'll get over it. I think he's at a point where he just wants everybody to go away so Forgotten Lake can get back to normal and he can go fishing again without anyone bothering him."

He nodded. "Maybe that's what everyone should do. Stop what they're doing and just go fishing."

"Maybe. But at a different lake, please. Any lake but Forgotten Lake."

CHAPTER 22

*C*ass sipped her morning coffee on the deck and looked happily out on a serene Forgotten Lake. There was a late summer chill in the air and mist rose from the calm water, but she felt the sun's growing warmth, a warmth that would soon burn the mist away, leading to a gorgeous day. It was a scene that always brought happiness, but on this day there were even more reasons to be happy. For starters, there was the hope that cooler heads would indeed prevail and defuse the militia standoff peacefully. Adding to that hopefulness was her father's change in attitude. He no longer blamed the government for every trouble and was actually accepting some responsibility himself. She looked across the table to where he sat, coffee mug in hand. He still seemed rather glum— no one would mistake his mood for giddiness—but he was showing signs of emerging from the deep funk he had sunk into following the shoot-out. More than anything, though, Cass's happiness that day rose from the memory of her lovemaking with Brian the night before on the island. The island, always special to Cass, now claimed an even deeper place in her heart. The rational economist in her warned that her growing love for Brian wasn't really the cure for all that troubled Forgotten Lake, but on this beautiful morning, basking in the memory of the previous night, it truly seemed so.

Jack put down his coffee mug on the table and looked over at Cass. "What time did you come in last night, anyway?"

"It was after midnight."

"Hmph, musta been some picnic."

Cass just smiled and Jack said, "I suppose Walsh'll be hanging around here again today."

"Good chance," she said. "You should probably get used to it."

"Hmph."

They lapsed into silence and after a few moments, the crunch of tires on gravel sounded from the back of the house followed by the slamming of car doors. "You expecting someone?" she asked.

"Nope. Could that be Walsh already?"

She shook her head. "I don't think so. He's supposed to be at work." She stood and started for the house but then she froze, astonished, as two people came around the corner and stepped onto the deck. It was her mother and Gentleman Gerald.

* * *

Brian Walsh was once more struggling to focus on the work spread across his desk. Images from the night before—Cass frolicking naked in the water, Cass sprawled across the blanket—all made concentration nearly impossible. He kept trying, though, because the work at hand was important. He had begun gathering information for Jack Baird's dam permit application. He had long held the view that a dam on Forgotten Lake's Bumble River outlet had environmental merit, but within the past few days it had become more than a mere technical issue. For Brian, it was now a matter of the heart.

Zack Buchwald walked up to Brian's desk. "You working on that dam permit for Forgotten Lake?"

Brian nodded.

"Well, forget it. It ain't gonna happen."

Brian sat back, shocked. "What the hell, Zack, the application hasn't even been submitted yet. How can you say it's not gonna happen?"

"Because it's not."

"Says who?"

"Says the Soil and Water Conservation District board, that's who. The board met in special session last night and voted unanimously against any dam on the Bumble."

"How come I wasn't told about the meeting?" Brian asked.

Zack shrugged. "Things can happen around here without your knowledge or approval. And the board has the final say, you know that."

"Not necessarily," Brian said. "This is arbitrary and capricious. It could easily be argued that it denies Jack Baird due process. The courts just might have something to say about it."

"If I want legal advice, I'll talk to a lawyer," Zack said. "And as a matter of fact, I did just that. I ran it by the assistant county attorney, and he determined that because of all the illegal stuff that's been going on out there, we're justified in not considering the application."

"But Jack was told in negotiations yesterday with government officials, including me as a representative of this district, that he could submit an application and that it would be given due consideration. Hell, we're going back on our word, Zack."

"Look, Brian, just drop it, okay? It's not gonna happen."

Brian's eyes narrowed. "Hey, Zack, what's really going on here?"

"I told you. The board met and decided. No dam. It's a done deal. *Finito.*"

"Who called the meeting?"

"Um ... I did."

"Zack, was Roscoe Dugan at the meeting by any chance?"

Zack hesitated. "Oh, what the hell, you'll find out anyway. Yeah, No Sweat was there. And, yeah, he's the one who insisted on calling the meeting, but that's not gonna change anything. The board acted. It's done, and if you value your job, you'll accept that."

"And I suppose you expect me to tell Jack that there's no point in submitting an application because it's already been denied?"

Zack shrugged. "Somebody's gotta tell him."

* * *

It was possible, Cass thought, that she had been in a situation this awkward before, but she couldn't recall it. The four of them—Cass, her father, her mother, and Gerald—were seated around the deck table. The conversation so far had been strained and halting. Jack's contribution had been mostly one- or two-word responses mixed with grunts and scowls. Diane Baird wasn't saying much either, and she had the look of a woman who'd been asked to climb into a snake pit. Only Gerald seemed eager to be about the business at hand. He was, after all, a man on a mission, but he also seemed aware that he was treading on hazardous emotional ground. He was dressed for his mission in brown jodhpurs with shiny black riding boots that came up almost to his knees, and a khaki safari shirt, complete with epaulets. A heavy gold chain around his neck sparkled from beneath the open shirt collar.

"I know this is an imposition, and a rather uncomfortable one at that," Gerald now explained, "but when the governor calls, one must put aside personal ease and do one's duty."

Jack glared with narrowed eyes. "Yeah, I suppose one must. And just what is it that the governor sent you here to do?"

"I'm primarily on a fact-finding mission, to gather information, as it were," Gerald said.

"He's the governor's emissary," Diane Baird added. "They're old friends and the governor values Gerald's judgment."

Gerald smiled and patted Diane's hand. "You make it sound as if I alone have the governor's ear, but that's simply not the case. In a crisis such as this, the governor tries to get input from numerous sources so that he can make informed decisions. I'm merely one of those sources, though I have had the honor of serving in this capacity before. There is a measure of trust involved, so I take my mission quite seriously."

Cass and Jack exchanged quick glances and Jack rolled his eyes as Gerald continued. "In addition to fact-finding, the governor has also asked, should the opportunity present itself, that I deal directly with the militia in pursuit of an amicable resolution."

Jack nodded. "Yeah, amicable would be good. Why don't you just work with the cops? They're already here and it's their job."

"Of course. Law enforcement is an essential component of the mission, and they've shown both professionalism and restraint so far, but ..." Gerald paused to flash a knowing smile. "But the governor likes to explore all options, and he believes, and I very much concur, that back channels can often be more productive in matters such as this."

Jack winced. "Can you say that again in plain English?"

Gerald laughed. "Surely. Mr. Baird, I'm asking for your help in making contact with the militia with the hope of defusing the crisis, a hope you must certainly share."

"They got all the roads blocked off," Jack said.

"I understand," Gerald said. "I also understand you have a boat and that the militia's campsite is on the very edge of the lake."

"So you want me to take you down there in my boat?"

"Think of it, Mr. Baird, as the governor asking. I'm merely his representative."

Jack eyed him for a long moment. "Aw, what the hell, I'll run you down there. Then nobody can say that I ain't done my duty."

Gerald smiled. "On behalf of the governor, sir, I thank you."

"And now *my* duty is done," said Diane Baird. Everyone looked at her as she continued. "I swore I'd never come back to this god-awful lake. I only did today because Gerald asked for my help, but now I have no intention of spending one more minute here than I have to. Come along, Cassandra, you and I are going into Forsythe for lunch."

"Um, under the circumstances, I think I should stay around here," Cass said.

"Nonsense," Diane said. "We're going to lunch and that's all there is to it."

* * *

129

After Cass and her mother left, Jack stood alone with Gerald on the deck as Gerald took in the scene as if for the first time. "Lovely place you have here," he said.

Jack shrugged. "My ex obviously doesn't think so."

Gerald smiled. "Well, you know how it is. Sometimes the ladies just see things differently."

"And you know how the ladies see things, huh?"

Gerald seemed to sense the awkwardness of the moment. "Perhaps we should get on with the mission."

"You sure you wanna go down there?"

"Absolutely."

"You know, the last time I tried to help someone contact the militia, a guy got shot."

"Yes, I'm aware of that," Gerald said, "but when the governor calls in difficult times, one must have a stout heart."

Jack eyed Gerald for a long moment as he considered telling him what he could do with his stout heart; then he simply shrugged and pointed to the dock. "Alright, let's go."

As they walked, Jack's regret grew for having agreed to take Gerald in his boat. It annoyed him that his ex had barged back into his life, and it was even more annoying that she had shown up with the guy she was shacked up with. But mostly it galled him that he'd been cuckolded by a scrawny little guy in funny pants. He glanced at Gerald now and shook his head. Some emissary. The militia would probably take one look at his pants and fall down laughing. Then another thought occurred to Jack, a malevolent one: accidents happen in boats. People fall out of them and drown. Jack shook his head. *With my luck, the son of a bitch'd probably swim like a fish.*

At the dock, Jack climbed down into the boat but before he could direct Gerald into the front seat, he heard another boat coming across the lake. Jack looked up to see Dup Dingle's boat approaching. Dup slowed and bumped against the dock and Jack smiled. Maybe he didn't have to take Gerald in his boat, after all.

CHAPTER 23

*O*nce again Brian Walsh's drive out to Forgotten Lake was angst-ridden. It seemed that every time things turned toward the bright side—as with his relationship with Cass—past troubles would rear up again and drag him back to the dark side—as with Jack Baird's dam. And it wasn't really fair to fault the dam. People were at fault; people like Commissioner Roscoe Dugan, who treated county government like a personal fiefdom, and Zack Buchwald, who lacked the courage to stand up to people like Dugan. But where was his own courage, Brian thought ruefully. He hadn't stood up to people like Dugan and Zack either, and now he was dutifully driving to Forgotten Lake to tell Jack that his application had been denied before it had even been submitted. He wasn't looking forward to Jack's reaction, but in truth he was even more worried about Cass's. He wanted to appear strong in her eyes, but he feared that his news would cast him as a wimp.

Arriving at the lake, he parked next to Jack's pickup and Cass's car. At least they were both there so he would only have to explain about the dam once. He took a deep breath, climbed out of his pickup, and walked around to the front where he stepped on the deck and knocked on the French doors.

Jack opened the door, his expression far from welcoming, but he did step back and allow Brian to enter. Once inside he looked around for Cass, and when he didn't see her, he turned back to Jack who said, "She ain't here."

"But ... her car's out back."

"She's with her mother. They went to lunch."

This came as a surprise to Brian. Cass had told him of her mother's vow to never return to Forgotten Lake, but now she was here nonetheless.

"They should be back soon," Jack said, "if you wanna wait."

"Um, actually I need to talk to you," Brian said. "I've got some news ... some unfortunate news."

Jack snorted. "What other kind is there?"

Brian explained about the board's decision to deny a dam permit for Forgotten Lake and concluded by saying, "I'm really sorry about this. It isn't at all what you were told would happen, and if you choose to pursue it, you might have legal recourse."

"Might, huh?" Jack shook his head. "You ever hear that expression 'You can't fight city hall'?"

Brian could only shrug and in the ensuing silence he heard the sound of car doors slamming from behind the house; moments later Cass and Diane Baird walked in. Introductions were made and Diane paused for a critical up-and-down appraisal. "So this is your charming engineer," she said.

"Mother!" Cass glared daggers.

"Not bad," Diane allowed. "Certainly better than one might expect to find anywhere near this god-awful lake."

"Mother, that's enough!"

Brian was beginning to blush at the attention as Diane looked around the room, then turned to Jack. "Where's Gerald?"

Jack shrugged. "Down with the militia, I suppose."

"You suppose? You just left him down there?"

"Who's Gerald?" Brian asked.

Jack nodded at Diane. "Her new boyfriend."

Diane glared at Jack. "He's the governor's emissary, and he happens to be here in an official capacity."

"Emissary?" Brian looked confused. "What's going on here?"

They ignored him and Diane said, "Jack Baird, do you mean to tell me that you left Gerald to fend for himself with those people?"

"Not exactly."

"What's that supposed to mean?"

"It means I didn't take him down there in the first place," Jack said.

"But ... but you sat right here and said you would."

"And I was gonna," Jack explained, "but when we got down to the dock, Dup came along in his boat, so I sent Gerald off with him instead."

Diane's eyes widened with horror. "You ... you sent the governor's emissary off in a boat with ... Dup Dingle?"

"Why not?" Jack said. "Dup can find the south end of the lake as good as me. Besides, I figured any emissary worth his salt oughta be able to look out for himself."

Diane's eyes narrowed menacingly now. "Jack, if anything happens to Gerald, you're going to be in so much trouble."

"Aw, hell," said Jack, "what's the worst thing that can happen? Maybe Dup'll take the emissary over to his cabin and let him poke his moss box."

"What?" Confusion clouded Diane's face.

Jack chuckled. "Then again, that might be a problem if it turns out he likes it better'n what he's currently poking."

"Jack, what on earth are you talking about?"

"Never mind," Jack said. "And quit all your damn worrying. The emissary'll be fine with Dup."

At that moment, as if on cue, Dup Dingle appeared outside, stepping up onto the deck. Alone.

* * *

Cass had long understood her mother's contempt for her father's minions, but the fury she was now venting on Dup Dingle reached a new level.

"And you just went off and left him there?" Diane was incredulous. "How could you be so stupid?"

Dup flinched and tried to back away, but Diane had him trapped against the table. "Weren't my idea," he said meekly.

"Yeah," said Jack, "don't go blaming Dup. Going down there and working that back-channel thing was Gerald's idea in the first place."

Diane paused to glare at Jack before turning once more on Dup. "Tell me exactly what happened."

Dup jammed his hands in his pockets and looked down, avoiding eye contact with his tormentor. "Well, I took him down there just like Jack told me to, and them militia fellas were right there on the shore with their guns like they was waiting for us. I says maybe we oughtn't go in, but that Gerald fella, he was set on it, so I beached her and he climbed outta the boat and right away them militia fellas kinda surrounded him."

"Dear God," said Diane.

"Did they laugh at his pants?" Jack asked.

Diane gave another withering look. "Shut up, Jack!"

"Nobody was laughing," Dup said. "They all looked kinda mad."

"Why did you leave?" Diane demanded.

"Because that head militia fella told me to git," Dup said, "and I wasn't about to argue with him. And that Gerald fella, he told me to go too."

"Oh, my God," Diane said. "We've got to do something."

"Did Gerald think to notify anyone, like the authorities, before he went off on his little mission?" Cass asked. "Does anyone else know he's down there with the militia?"

Diane shook her head. "I don't think so. The governor knows, of course—he's the one who sent Gerald up here—but I don't think he talked to anyone else."

"I'll call the sheriff's office in Forsythe," Brian said. "They're kind of the central clearing house on this deal and they can get word to everyone who needs to know."

"Sheriff's office!" Diane was getting more upset by the moment. "What can those fools do? Call the National Guard! Call the governor, for God's sake!"

"Now don't get yourself all in a panic," Jack said. "Times like this call for calm and level-headed thinking."

"And true patriots," said a voice from the open French doors. They had been so caught up in their discussion that they hadn't noticed anyone coming onto the deck and they all turned now to find Hamilton Madison standing there.

* * *

"You been down to the militia camp today?" Jack asked.

Hamilton Madison shook his head. "No, but I'm on my way down there now. I stopped by here because you're going with me."

Ham's statement sounded a good deal like an order, and Cass exchanged questioning looks with Brian. She had always thought Ham strange, but on this day, dressed in his usual camo and with his holstered sidearm once more strapped around his waist, he looked dangerous, and the tone of his voice did nothing to lessen that feeling.

Jack didn't seem to pick up on Ham's tone, though, as he said, "Yeah, I just might go down there with you. It's time the militia packed up and got outta here, and I intend to tell 'em so."

"Not gonna happen," Ham said.

"What the hell you talking about?" Jack said. "It's my land, and if I say go, then by God they'll go or else."

Ham calmly shook his head. "They're not going anywhere, Jack. They're committed. These are hard men and they won't back down till they see it through to victory."

"And just what will a victory look like?" Cass asked.

Ham glared at her and said, "When the goddamn government starts obeying the Constitution and we get our country back, that's what victory'll look like." With those words, he turned back to Jack. "But in the meantime you gotta secede."

Jack blinked with astonishment. "I gotta what?"

"Secede. Leave the country."

"I ain't going nowhere," Jack said.

"Not you, the lake," Ham said. "Forgotten Lake has to secede from the United States."

After a moment of stunned silence, Jack shook his head. "You've gone fucking nuts!"

Dup Dingle's face was a mask of confusion. "How you gonna move a lake?"

They ignored Dup's question and Cass said, "This is ridiculous. To begin with, you've got no legal standing to waltz in here and demand anything, much less a secession."

Ham sneered. "The government violating the Constitution is all the legal standing we need. The militia is the last line of defense against tyranny."

Cass wasn't buying it. "How would you even go about seceding?"

Her question briefly stumped Ham. "Um ... I suppose you start out with some kinda declaration."

"You mean like the Declaration of Independence?"

"Yeah," Ham said, then immediately thought better of it. "No, a different kind of declaration. A declaration of secession maybe." After another moment's thought, he added, "Major Mike'll know how to do it. Texans are experts when it comes to seceding."

"I don't give a flying fuck what they do in Texas," Jack said. "I ain't seceding from nothing and that's that!"

"Oh, yes you are, Jack." With that Hamilton Madison drew his pistol and aimed it at Jack's chest. "My boat's tied up to your dock, so just come along with me and we'll have us a nice little boat ride."

CHAPTER 24

*S*upervising Deputy Hank Cross wanted his life back; he wanted to go fishing, something he hadn't done in over a week, largely because of the Forgotten Lake fiasco. And the prospects for sneaking out to wet a line anytime soon were bleak so long as the area sheriff's office in Forsythe remained a command bunker for federal and state cops. There was no escaping the hubbub with Black of ATF and White of BCA directing their agents from a large table just outside Hank's office. Assistant County Attorney Green was in and out too, as were the extra deputies sent up from Duluth by Sheriff Brown. As for the sheriff himself, he had returned to Duluth, but now he was calling almost hourly for updates. Yes, confusion reigned at the Forsythe office, but since most of those involved were law enforcement professionals, there was an underlying order to the confusion, a cop calm beneath the disorder, a calm that went completely missing whenever the biggest pain in the ass appeared: Commissioner Roscoe Dugan. When Dugan wasn't in the office demanding one thing or another, he was making wild, unsubstantiated claims to the media about anarchy at Forgotten Lake. Black and White had lost all patience with the commissioner and wanted to come down hard on him, but Hank had cautioned against it. After all, when this was finally over the agents could walk away and forget Forgotten Lake, but Hank would have to live with Dugan.

Deputy Carter Dilworth stuck his head through the open door of Hank's office. "Can you take the call on line two, Hank?"

Dilworth had been assigned to administrative desk duty since his run-in with Jack Baird, or as Sheriff Brown had succinctly put it, "Don't let that son of a bitch anywhere near the public." Hank looked wearily at the stack of reports he was working through and said, "Can't Sam Skinner take it?"

"Sam's out on a call. And I think you wanna take this one anyway."

"Who is it?"

"Brian Walsh. He's out at Forgotten Lake."

Hank sighed. "Alright." He reached for the phone but before picking it up he noticed Dilworth still craning through the doorway. He pointed a finger at the deputy and said, "Get the hell outta here!" Dilworth was gone in a wink and Hank picked up the phone. Three minutes later he cradled it again and shook his head. Prospects for wetting a line were getting bleaker by the moment. He got up from his desk and walked to the door where he called to Black and White at their table. "Could you gentlemen join me in here?"

* * *

Hamilton Madison had expected a more enthusiastic response from Major Mike. After all, it was Major Mike who had brought up the idea of secession in the first place, but now both he and Wanda seemed to be hedging. They were seated on logs by the campfire. Fifty feet away Jack and Gerald sat on the ground, each leaning against a different tree. They were guarded by a militiaman with an automatic rifle.

"I thought you were all for secession," Ham said now.

Major Mike nodded. "I am ... in principle. But Jack's the landowner and you had to bring him in here at gunpoint, so he's clearly not on board with secession. That's a problem."

"Maybe we could, like, persuade him," Ham said.

"You mean like torture him?" Wanda said. "Bad, bad idea."

Ham nodded in the direction of Jack and Gerald. "So what about them? Just let 'em go?"

Major Mike pondered a moment. "No, for now anyway I think we should keep them here as our ... guests. Even if they're not supporting the cause, they can still be useful."

"How's that?"

"Well, for one thing, the law's less likely to throw a bunch of firepower at us as long as they're here. And secondly, the governor's guy there might come in handy with communicating our demands."

Ham nodded; then his face clouded with confusion. "We have demands?"

Major Mike nodded solemnly.

"Like what?"

"Not sure yet," Major Mike said, "but they'll probably include some kind of immunity from prosecution."

Ham could hardly believe his ears. "You wanna cut a deal?"

"And maybe a cash settlement too," Major Mike added.

"Cash settlement? You want 'em to give you money?"

Major Mike shrugged. "It's not cheap running a militia. There's weapons and ammo and living expenses. It adds up."

"And I wanna go to Hawaii this winter," said Wanda.

Hamilton Madison was shaken to his core. The thought of true patriots selling out for money went against everything he believed, though his shock was tempered a bit by the idea of Wanda stretched out on a beach. In his mind's eye her bikini was skimpy and done in camo.

* * *

"Jack Baird kidnapped?" Black was shocked.

"Hamilton Madison?" said White. "Isn't he the conspiracy nut that lives across the lake from Baird?"

Hank Cross nodded. "The same. We thought he was harmless, but I guess you never know with these types."

"And what about this guy the governor supposedly sent up here?" Black asked. "What'd you call him? An emissary? And why the hell weren't we told about him?"

Hank could only shrug. "Apparently, the governor sent him here on some kind of special mission. They're old friends, I guess."

"Helluva way to treat a friend," Black said. "And this mission, was part of it to go in there and get his ass taken hostage?"

Another shrug from Hank.

"What a goddamn mess!" Black shook his head; then he turned to White. "You're the state guy here. I'm gonna let you advise the governor about this latest fuckup."

"Thanks a lot," said White with an obvious lack of gratitude.

"And I don't like doing it," Black said, "but I think it's time to mobilize the Guard and move them into position."

"You think that's wise?" White asked.

"There's nothing wise about this whole goddamn operation, but I think we gotta do it. If Forgotten Lake blows up, we gotta be ready to deal with it."

"Forgotten Lake's blowing up?" The question came from the open doorway and they turned to find Roscoe Dugan standing there.

"I said 'if,' Commissioner," Black said. "We're just talking about prudent precautions."

"Prudent precautions, my ass!" said Dugan. "I say send 'em in there today and put an end to this cluster fuck."

"How long've you been standing there, Commissioner?" Hank asked.

"Long enough to know that they've taken hostages now and that one of 'em is an emissary from the governor. Good God, what more reason do you people need to finally get off your asses and act?"

"Not gonna happen," Black said. "For one thing, there's a hundred yards of thick woods between the road and their camp. That gives them a lot of cover, so any attempt to force our way in is bound to get awful bloody."

"Then put the Guard in boats and attack 'em from the lake," Dugan said.

"Are you nuts?" White was incredulous.

Dugan glared at the BCA agent. "No, I'm not nuts. I'm thinking boldly, something you people oughta start doing. And, yeah, an amphibious assault may be just the sort of bold move that'll catch 'em off guard."

Black'd had enough. "They'll see them coming from two hundred yards out. They'll be sitting ducks! This is not fucking Iwo Jima, Commissioner, and you're not fucking Admiral Nimitz!"

Dugan glowered. "So you're gonna just sit here and do nothing?"

"No," said Black. "We'll move the Guard in close, but not at the site, so they'll be available if we need them, but there'll be no attack as long as there's a chance to negotiate a peaceful outcome."

Hank Cross sighed. Fishing remained a distant hope.

* * *

Brian climbed into the bow of the boat and pushed off from the dock as Cass pulled the starter cord on the outboard motor. The motor sputtered to life on the third pull and she then throttled down as they slowly motored out into the lake. He looked back at her. "You sure this is a good idea?"

"I had to get out of the house before my mother drove me crazy," Cass said.

"I can understand getting out of the house," he said, "but paying a visit to the militia seems a bit rash. What makes you think we'll get a different reception than Gerald did?"

Rather than answering, Cass turned the boat onto a heading for the north end of the island.

Brian looked around, confused. "Um, not that I necessarily disapprove, but aren't you going the wrong way? The militia camp's down there," he said, pointing to the south.

"I'm not stupid," she said. "We're not sailing in like Gerald, hoping for a warm welcome. I grew up on this lake. I know every inch of it, and I also know all the trails around it. I think we can get close without them knowing we're there."

"And then what?"

She shrugged. "And then we'll see what we see."

He shook his head. "You may have a PhD in economics, but right now you're thinking like your old man."

She smiled and turned the boat southward as they rounded the northern tip of the island.

* * *

Sitting on the ground, his back against a tree trunk, Jack Baird looked over to where Gerald sat in a similar pose. The governor's emissary seemed calm, almost serene, which struck Jack as odd, given their circumstances. He was beginning to suspect that the man wasn't completely in touch with reality, a notion further supported by Gerald's goofy pants, not to mention his taste in women. Then to Jack's surprise, Gerald looked up at the militiaman guarding them and asked, "Do you suppose we might have some water?"

The militiaman stared impassively for a long moment before giving a curt nod. "Yeah, I'll get you some water, but don't get any ideas about going anywhere. I'm just going over to the camp kitchen there and I'll be watching you the whole time." The militiaman stared icily for another moment, as if to emphasize his watchfulness; then he slowly walked away, looking back over his shoulder every few steps.

Jack looked at Gerald again and asked, "So how's the back-channel negotiating working out?" It was a taunting question, but given their current straits, he thought Gerald worthy of a taunt or two, though Gerald didn't seem to take it as one.

"Quite well, actually," Gerald said. "Things seem to be falling into place rather nicely, I think."

That settled it for Jack. The man really was unmoored from reality. "We're sitting here on the ground, guarded by a guy with an automatic rifle, and you think it's going quite well?"

"I wouldn't place too much importance on our present circumstances," Gerald said. "It's a rather fluid situation, and though it may not seem like it, we do have considerable leverage. I do worry about that Madison fellow, though. He seems rather a loose cannon."

The militiaman returned with two plastic bottles of water, tossing them onto the ground between Jack and Gerald. Gerald reached for the bottles, gave one to Jack, then leaned against his tree again, sipping water as if he hadn't a care in the world.

A minute later Major Mike walked up and stood in front of them. He stared wordlessly at Jack for a moment; then he turned to Gerald. "I think it's time we talk."

Gerald nodded. "Yes, I quite agree."

Well, I'll be damned, thought Jack.

* * *

They motored slowly down the east side of the island. Cass kept the outboard throttled down to minimize the noise and avoid drawing attention to their presence on the lake. They cruised past Hamilton Madison's cabin, then a little farther on past Dup Dingle's humble shack. Just as they cleared the southern tip of the island and vehicles and tents in the militia camp came into view in the distance, she turned onto an easterly heading. Brian peered ahead. Cass seemed to know where she was going but all Brian saw was solid woods along a rocky shoreline. He looked back at her and turned up both palms in a gesture of inquiry but she ignored him, concentrating instead on steering the boat. Then at fifty yards he saw a break in the rocks and a patch of sandy beach. A minute later she cut the engine and they skidded to a stop on the sand. He climbed out and she followed; then they pulled the boat farther onto the sand and tied it off to a tree.

"Now what?" Brian asked, looking about.

"Now we take the trail."

"What trail?"

"Follow me." With her arms up to fend away branches, she started inland with Brian behind and indeed after twenty feet they came to a narrow trail running parallel to the lake. "Told you," she said.

"Okay, so you're Mark Trail, but what's the plan?"

She pointed along the trail. "Let's follow this a bit and see what we see."

"There you go with 'see what we see' again. For Chrissakes, Cass, armed militia is down there. That's what we're likely to see, and more to the point, they're likely to see us."

"We won't get that close."

"Then why go?"

She turned to him. "Humor me, Brian. This is my lake, my home, and I don't like what's happening here. And my dad's being held hostage. I can't just stand by and do nothing."

He wasn't in a mood to humor her, but then she turned and started down the trail. He hesitated for a moment, then followed.

* * *

Dup Dingle was terrified. After Hamilton Madison led Jack off to the militia camp at gunpoint, he had returned to his shack where he had been cowering in fear ever since. The militia's presence at Forgotten Lake had upended his world. Jack had given some hope that they might leave soon, but now Jack himself was a prisoner of the militia. Jack Baird: Dup's chief source of order, the rock at the center of his life. If they could take Jack, then no one was safe at Forgotten Lake. Every few minutes Dup got up to peer warily out his front window, half expecting the militia or the cops or both to come for him next. Now as he looked out he was startled to see a boat passing by, Jack's boat, with Cass running the motor and that government fella sitting up front. They were heading down lake, toward the militia camp, and Dup's stomach knotted with dread. What were they doing? Did they want to be taken prisoner too?

Dup watched them go. It suddenly seemed as if the whole world was being drawn to the south end of Forgotten Lake where calamity surely awaited. And now Dup, too, felt calamity's pull. He feared it greatly, but his world was at risk; Jack was in danger, and now Cass might be as well. He wasn't sure what he could do, but he had to do something. He opened the door and stepped out onto the stoop, staring down lake, summoning courage from some unknown place. He went back into the shack and took his shotgun down from where it hung on the wall; then he walked to the cupboard that held his bread and coffee and Little Debbies and on the top shelf his shotgun shells. He reached for a box and looked at it. No. 4 shot, a duck load. He put it back and took another box. BBBs, a goose load. Better. He loaded three shells into the gun, put three more in his pocket, then walked outside and down to his boat.

* * *

A black Yukon with government plates came to a stop where the road crossed the Bumble River just south of Forgotten Lake. Agents Black and White climbed out and stood next to the vehicle, looking cautiously about. They were waiting for Hank Cross. Once the supervising deputy arrived, they planned to hail the militia with a bullhorn, propose a truce, and try to get a dialogue started. It bore considerable risk; the militia had proved to be unpredictable, but they were desperate. The longer the standoff went on, the greater the chance of a bloody disaster.

The sound of an approaching vehicle came through the still air and they looked up the road. "That must be Cross now," said White.

A moment later a Humvee painted in camo crested the hill, followed by another, then another, six in all. "Aw, shit!" said Black. "It's the goddamn Guard. They were supposed to wait back at the last crossroad."

White shook his head. "One fuckup after another."

The lead Humvee came to a stop next to the agents. A sergeant was behind the wheel, a captain in the passenger seat. Both men had camo-painted their faces to match their uniforms and vehicle. The captain leaned out his window. "Where you want us?"

Black pointed angrily up the road. "A mile back that way. You were only supposed to come in if you were called. Who the hell sent you in?"

"A guy who said he was a county commissioner," the captain said. "He said you wanted us in ASAP."

"That son of a bitch!" said Black.

The captain seemed startled by the agent's anger. "You want us to pull back?"

Black looked toward the woods, thought a moment, then shook his head. "Nah, it's too late for that. Their sentries are sure to have seen you. Pull back now and it'll just add to the confusion. Better to keep everything in the open where they can see it. But keep your weapons outta sight. And don't do anything that might look aggressive or threatening." He turned to White. "Okay, let's see if we can get some dialogue going before people start shooting again."

* * *

Hamilton Madison was growing more disgusted by the moment when Gerald said to Major Mike, "I'm confident that can be arranged, but we have to act promptly, and there can be no more gunfire."

They were seated on logs around the smoldering campfire. Gerald was on one side with Jack sitting glumly to his right. Across the fire sat Major Mike, flanked by Wanda and a glowering Hamilton Madison. For the past fifteen minutes they had been discussing terms of disengagement whereby the militia could walk away without fear of prosecution so long as they did so quickly and peacefully. Major Mike and Gerald had done most of the talking.

"It's helpful that there've been no fatalities and only one minor casualty," Gerald added now. "It also augurs in your favor that until recently you've occupied this site with the owner's permission."

Jack gave a derisive snort that the others ignored.

"And the money?" Major Mike asked.

Ham cringed. *You're not true patriots. You're nothing but goddamn money-grubbing mercenaries!*

"That might be a bit trickier," Gerald said. "It certainly can't come out of the state's general fund, but that's not to say there aren't some, um ... special funds that might be tapped. I'll have to make some phone calls."

"But we're not leaving until that part's settled," said Major Mike. "If we do, we lose our leverage."

"I understand," said Gerald. "Let's at least communicate your willingness to leave, pending negotiations. That would help cool things off and create a better atmosphere for talks going forward."

The walkie-talkie on the ground next to Major Mike squawked. He picked it up, spoke into it, then listened, and after that he said, "Roger." He put it down and looked at the others. "Looks like we won't have to go looking for them to get talks started. That was Mack out on picket. He says there're two guys on the road who look like cops."

"Excellent," Gerald said. "No time like the present to start negotiations."

There was movement to one side and they all turned to see Cass and Brian walking toward them, a militiaman with an automatic rifle marching behind them.

"What the hell?" said Jack.

"What've we got here, Zeke?" Major Mike asked.

"Found these two snooping around in the woods," Zeke, said. "Figured I'd escort 'em in so we could find out what they're up to."

"That's my daughter," Jack said. "You harm one hair on her head and there'll be hell to pay!"

"What about him?" Major Mike said, pointing at Brian.

"Him you can shoot."

"Dad!" Cass said, glaring at her father.

The walkie-talkie squawked again. Major Mike picked it up, keyed it, and said, "Yeah, Mack." Then he listened and as he did he turned to glare at Gerald. After a few moments, he said, "Hold your position, Mack, and stay outta sight. I'll get back to you ASAP." He put the walkie-talkie down, his gaze still fixed on Gerald. "Mack says the army's out there on the road now. He counts six Humvees. What the hell's going on? Is this how you negotiate?"

Suddenly Gerald seemed less confident. "I ... I don't know anything about that. The governor did put a special National Guard unit on alert, but I'm sure he wouldn't have ordered them in without provocation on your part, and you haven't done that."

"Well, they're here and in force," Major Mike said. "I have to assume they're getting ready to attack." He reached for the walkie-talkie again.

"No, no," Gerald pleaded. "It's got to be a mistake, some kind of screw-up. You're right though, the situation is explosive. We need to act fast. I propose that you and I walk out there right now under a white flag of truce. We've got to start talking to them. It's our only chance to defuse this thing before it blows up in our faces."

White flag of truce! Hamilton Madison was filled with sudden rage. The army appearing out on the road had been cause for joy. His moment of glory had come. Armageddon at last! But now to his horror Major Mike was contemplating a truce with the very tyrants bent on destroying the Constitution. Ham felt glory slipping from his grasp, not to mention redemption for shitting his pants.

Major Mike looked down at the walkie-talkie in his hand and pondered the situation; then he nodded and stood up. "Okay, let's do it." He turned to Wanda, "Get me something white to use as the flag."

Wanda went quickly to the camper she shared with Major Mike as Ham's mood grew darker and darker. What a sorry day it was turning into for patriotism. Hamilton and Madison were surely spinning in their graves. Wanda returned with something white that she handed to Major Mike.

He held it up and did a double take. "Panties?"

She shrugged. "Everything else is camo. And I want those back!"

There it was, the final horror, thought Ham. They were about to surrender to tyrants under a white flag of panties. Something snapped in his brain.

Major Mike found a suitable stick and tied Wanda's panties to it; then he turned to Gerald. "Okay, let's—"

A loud burst of automatic rifle fire shattered the air.

Everyone turned. Hamilton Madison stood there, his rifle pointing skyward, the smell of cordite heavy in the air. Slowly, deliberately, he lowered the gun and aimed it at Major Mike's chest. "Ain't gonna be no surrender today. We're gonna fight, and we'll fight to the death if we have to!"

* * *

After the burst of gunfire sounded from the woods, Black and White exchanged looks of dismay; then both men dove for the road ditch. Men were piling out of the Humvees, their weapons out and ready for action. The Guard captain ordered them to take cover in the ditch as well; then he dove in next to Black and White. "What's the plan?" he asked.

Plan? Black could only shake his head. "Just keep down. And no one fires unless we're actually fired on!" He stared glumly across the road into the woods. Some plan, he thought, wishing he'd never heard of Forgotten Lake.

* * *

Upon hearing gunfire coming from shore, Dup Dingle was seized by fear. He had been drifting along with the motor off, peering intently into the militia camp from a hundred yards out. At that distance he'd been unable to see much, and part of him wanted to go in closer while the rest of him cried out for a hasty retreat to the safety of his shack. A ways up the shore he had passed Jack's boat, beached with no one around. It was then that he had shut the motor down and started drifting as he imagined the dire straits Cass might have stumbled into. But now gunfire had sounded from the camp. The time for imagining was over. His friends were surely in trouble, and as much as he wanted to flee, he couldn't desert them now. He pulled the starter cord and the outboard sputtered to life; then he throttled down and steered for shore, reaching with his free hand for the shotgun.

149

* * *

For the first time, Jack Baird was gripped by sudden and intense fear. Until now it had all felt like a game, at times an angry game, but still a game he could simply call off when reason said it was time to stop playing. But there was no reason in Hamilton Madison's wild, darting eyes, only madness. He looked to where Cass and Brian stood in each other's arms, embraces that would offer scant protection should bullets start flying. Jack instinctively moved sideways two steps, placing himself in the line of fire between Ham and his daughter. Still not a lot of protection, but some; then he summoned his most commanding voice, though it came out with a quiver. "Put the gun down, Ham! Now!"

"Fuck you, Jack!"

"He's right, Madison," Major Mike said. "Put it down before you do something you'll regret."

"Fuck you too," said Ham. "You're one sorry damn excuse for a patriot and you've got no business telling me what to do!" His rifle was still aimed at Major Mike, and while several militiamen looked on, no one raised a weapon for fear of getting their leader shot. Everyone seemed to understand that they were dealing with a madman.

Then Jack saw Dup Dingle coming up behind Ham from the shore, inching stealthily along with a shotgun in his hands. He had no idea what Dup had in mind, but he thought it best to keep Ham talking. "A real patriot wouldn't be doing this, Ham," he said. "A real patriot would wanna talk things out. You're not acting like a patriot at all."

Ham's face contorted with rage. "Bullshit! I am too a patriot! I'm the only fucking patriot on this fucking lake!"

Dup was within ten yards of Ham now. He stopped, raised his gun, and yelled in a strained and fearful voice, "Drop it, Ham."

Hamilton Madison whirled around. "Dingle, you piece of shit!" He brought his rifle to bear on Dup just as Dup shouldered his shotgun. In the next instant both men fired simultaneously. In the instant following that both men crumpled to the ground.

No one moved in the stillness that followed, as if they were frozen with disbelief. Then belief slowly seeped through and Jack looked with horror at his minions, both facedown and silent on the ground, blood pooling beneath them.

EPILOGUE

*J*ack Baird sat in the back of his boat, fishing rod in hand, eyeing his bobber twenty feet away. On this mid-October day, the sky was overcast and Forgotten Lake lay flat and gray in a light breeze. Two weeks earlier the birch and maple trees had dazzled with fall brilliance, but now the leaves were mostly down, leaving bare limbs silhouetted darkly against the gray sky with only the muted green of pine trees offering much in the way of color contrast. Soon the lake would freeze over and the snow would come and the landscape would become even more monochromatic, but none of this bothered Jack. He loved Forgotten Lake in every season.

In the end, Jack had been forced to tear out his dam—you really can't fight city hall—but it had been a wet fall and Forgotten Lake had risen naturally to a good level. Jack took further satisfaction from Roscoe Dugan being denied any opportunity to gloat over his victory, given the public rebuke issued by ATF's Black, followed by an equally damning one from the governor's office. Before the Rumble on the Bumble, Dugan had been unopposed for reelection, but now a Methodist minister from Forsythe, pledging to restore integrity to county government, was mounting a write-in campaign to unseat the commissioner in November. Dugan was running scared as the preacher seemed to gain momentum each day, and the joke around Forsythe was that No Sweat really had something to sweat about this time.

153

In contrast to Dugan's rebuke from St. Paul, the governor had heaped high praise on his personal emissary, crediting Gerald with single-handedly ending the crisis and preventing further loss of life. Jack could only shake his head. The governor could believe that a skinny guy strutting around in funny pants had saved the day if he wanted to, but Jack had been there, and he saw things differently. No matter. More important was Diane Baird's declaration that she *absolutely* would never again be caught dead or alive at Forgotten Lake, so regular family reunions seemed a remote possibility, and Jack was fine with that.

The whole episode had done nothing to improve Jack's view of government and those who practice it, and now he shook his head at the thought of another politician whose star was actually rising because of the Forgotten Lake fiasco. Bolstered by huge financial support from the NRA, Clancy Meeker was now the odds-on favorite to beat longtime Congressman Clausen Diggs. Much of that funding had gone to purchase several thousand coonskin caps, which Meeker gleefully handed out to his supporters. Each cap had an embroidered patch sewn to the front that read: Elect Clancy Meeker! Make the Northland Great Again! Jack was disgusted by the whole business, but at least Meeker had the good sense to stay well clear of Forgotten Lake when campaigning.

So Forgotten Lake was at last rid of politicians, and Jack was equally thankful and relieved that it was once more militia free as well. In the wake of the fatal shootout, Major Mike and Wanda and the others couldn't get away fast enough—forgetting any thoughts of monetary incentive—and the authorities had been more than happy to see them go.

If there was a silver lining to all of that summer's storm clouds—and a surprising one, at that—it was Cass's decision to move back permanently. On the spur of the moment, she had resigned her position at Tulane and accepted a similar one at the University of Minnesota's Duluth campus where she now taught economics three days a week.

"So, they pay more money in Duluth?" Jack had asked when she announced her decision.

"Less, actually."

"Don't sound like very smart economics to me," Jack had teased, though he knew full well her real motivation. Oh, she yammered on about her soul's compass and her true north, but it was pretty hard to overlook her moving into Brian Walsh's small cabin on Round Lake.

"You gonna get married?" Jack asked.

Cass shrugged. "No plans for now. Bairds don't have a great history when it comes to marriage. I wouldn't want to jinx the relationship at the start."

Jack had to admit to the logic of that. Mostly, though, he was just delighted that he would be seeing more of his daughter, even if she was shacked up with a government guy. As for Walsh, Jack remained wary—a father's natural wariness of a daughter's lover—but he was beginning to warm a bit. After all, if Walsh was indeed the chief reason Cass had moved back, then there had to be something to like about the man.

Jack's bobber went down. He let the line play out and after ten feet or so it stopped. Walleye, he thought hopefully. A northern or a bass would still be going. He gave it a few more seconds to swallow the bait; then he slowly reeled in, feeling for the fish, and at the first tug he whipped the rod back, setting the hook, noting with satisfaction how sharply the rod bowed. Whatever it was, it had some size to it. The fish overrode the drag on the reel twice before Jack finally got it alongside the boat and got a look at it: a walleye, indeed, close to twenty inches. Holding the rod high, he grabbed the landing net and netted his catch.

"Nice one, Jack," Dup Dingle said from the bow.

"Yeah, I reckon it's a keeper."

Jack unhooked the fish and put it on his stringer; then he rebaited his hook. After recasting his line he looked over at Dup, who reeled in his own line to check his bait, and when he cast it out again Jack noticed him wince with pain. "That shoulder still hurting you quite a bit?" Jack asked.

"A bit," Dup said. "Getting better though. Doc said a bullet wound like mine's bound to bother a while, but I reckon I can live with that. Just glad they didn't charge me with nothing."

"Charge, hell! They shoulda given you a goddamn medal."

"Don't want no goddamn medal," Dup said. "Just wanna be left alone."

They lapsed into silence again, each minding his own bobber. After a few minutes a lone duck flew overhead. Jack pointed at it and said, "I'm thinking we oughta get our blind set up on the tip of the island there. Bluebills'll be down from Canada before long and we wanna be ready for them."

Dup hesitated before responding. "You know, Jack, I think I'm gonna pass on hunting this year."

"What the hell you talking about? We've been hunting together every year since I can't remember when."

Dup hesitated again. "It's just that ... I ain't never killed nobody before, and ever since I killed Ham, I ain't felt like shooting nothing else."

"Not even a duck?"

Dup shrugged, which caused him to wince with pain again. "Reckon I'll just stick to fishing for now." At that, his bobber went down. "Hey!"

CPSIA information can be obtained
at www.ICGtesting.com
Printed in the USA
FSOW01n0557050817
37241FS